# The Yellow Field

Books may be purchased in quantity and/or special sales by contacting the publisher. All inquiries related to such matters should be addressed to:

Middle Creek Publishing & Audio
9167 Pueblo Mountain Park Road
Beulah, CO 81023
editor@middlecreekpublishing.com
(719) 369-9050

First Paperback Edition, 2020
ISBN: 9781734820812

Cover Design: David Anthony Martin

Author photo: Tim Keller

# The Yellow Field

## Peter Edward Burg

Middle Creek Publishing & Audio
Beulah, CO

*for Patricia Burg Hughes*

# Chapters

**One**    Thursday, 12<sup>th</sup> Afternoon        1

**Two**    Wednesday, 11<sup>th</sup>        31

**Three** Thursday, 12<sup>th</sup>        67

**Four**   Thursday, 12<sup>th</sup> 1:15 PM        85

**Five**   Friday, 13<sup>th</sup>        117

**Six**    Friday, 13<sup>th</sup> Afternoon        141

**Seven** Saturday, 14<sup>th</sup> Morning        155

**Eight** Saturday, 14<sup>th</sup> Evening        177

**Nine**   Sunday, 15<sup>th</sup> Morning        183

**Ten**    Sunday, 15<sup>th</sup> Later        193

# One
## Thursday, 12th Afternoon

The yellow field was bright against the sky as the game of day began as if the field had gotten the better of the blue sky for an envious moment, a dry yellow that ran west along the shadow line of rich Douglas fir with shadowed patches of dark that drew the eye in and coaxed a distant memory of some forgotten doubt. This waiting field of yellow and green kissed before exploding into that cloudless sky, a sky of dappled tired dryness that seeped into the skin and clothes of anyone standing under it. It was an end of summer days that had left this field desperate and the unbelievable and believable rode on the light breath of fall.

The Wet Mountains are the eastern most range of the Rocky Mountains, and this high-altitude field is two-faced. One profile is jagged and eternal, created by the upheaval of continental clashes during the orogeny period or mountain building two million years ago. The other profile is ephemeral and pastel ever changing. An artist's touch. Molded, painted and carved by the nurturing hand of Mother Nature. Her handiwork shows patience and defines beauty. The two faces are the epitome of theater. The real and the absurd. Comedy and tragedy existing simultaneously struggling with each other back and forth throughout the march of eons. This field, the playground of light and dark, the burial ground of summer, winter, fall and spring, lives. It is the destination of dreams. The fulfillment of glory. The birthplace of truth. Home of the sublime secret. The fingerprint of all mankind will eventually vanish from its skin, as if a drop of rain on thirsty soil . . .

Clem was nettled that he had waited until now to cut this field. It was probably a waste of time. The seed had all scattered so late in the season. The habit was all there was. He looked at his puffy hands on the wheel then closed his eyes and felt the sun make fire under his collar. He rubbed the crimson wrinkles on the back of his neck. The skin had begun to resemble the lichen on rocks found along Rattlesnake Ridge. He heaved a sigh that was lost with the noise of the engine then lit a cigarette and muttered, "It's late." Clem gazed at the field. He blew smoke into the raw blue space above him. The smoke slowly whirled up and vanished. That could be why he so deliberately halted the tractor and stared off. The stare and he himself were momentarily lost and dissolved in and out of focus and consciousness. He so loved the suspended magic of daydreams with the sun's warmth baking his memories. His eyes closed and the red dazzle behind the lids reinforced everything about good. He opened his eyes and looked at Cuerno Verde's rugged vista, which he woke up to every morning, and the hills cascading down filled with fir, pine, spruce and aspen. He had looked at it a thousand times before, but today was slightly odd. He felt that crispness in the air that always precedes autumn. Like the brush of air when someone walks by. But then it was gone.

The angular boundaries of the ranch with its slopes and small valley were more inviting than when he first fell in love with it so many years ago. He was stunned by a sharp memory of looking at it with young eyes. Why he was cutting so late in the season nagged at him still. Clem hissed a laugh out between his teeth. "I sure as shit hope nobody is watching me," he spoke to himself. He rubbed and thought and shifted back in gear and rattled along.

Clem's recent behavior had him flummoxed. He watched the days fly by lickety-split. Even weeks were up and gone without a real grasp or acknowledgement of anything accomplished. Just gone. "Just god damn gone," as he had been saying so often lately.

Over the past several weeks he had compiled a mental list of ass-chappers. Leaving the lights on in the house all night. Leaving the dogs out till dawn to wander and howl. Letting the paint on the siding of the west side of the house peel off down to wood. Allowing the ragweed, Russian thistle and mullein to grow as high as the front gate. Putting up with a water heater that no longer functioned. Neglecting to clean and tune-up the chain saw and arrange for cutting winter wood. Was it a matter of forgetting or that he really didn't care anymore? Was it a matter of inspiration or necessity that got him out of bed each morning? What could he do and still enjoy? Was the list of things that he could both do and enjoy running out? He looked again at Cuerno Verde's timber line thinking...

Clem had lately been slacking off. That much was true. So what. So what if the dogs were out all night? They'd keep the damn bears away and sleep all day. He knew one thing for sure; it felt good to be out in God's country working the field with the sun warming him. He could run this tractor and let his thoughts drift. He was partial to anything that left him to his own device. He took people and things at his own peculiar pace. His need for uncrowded air was dire. *Maybe that was it*, he thought. That is the oddness that stuck to the air around him. Maybe he did not *like* the air around him any longer. Maybe there was the scent of something that had died, something no longer autonomous and this contraption he rode was just a connection to the past, a dream he had nurtured throughout his life. Only now it no longer matched his time, his place, or his life. *So what?*

Clem pinched his eyes shut and furrowed his brows. "Lots of wires getting crossed here," he whispered. It didn't have to be complicated. It could be as simple as the warmth from the sun, as light as magpies drafting on the wind. It could be the motion of a leaf floating to the ground, or changing sparkplugs, fixing a flat, or shoeing a horse. Clem's thoughts were starting to race again. Today's talk with himself *was* becoming complicated again, a virtual anthill of problems.

### *Wednesday, 11th*

Clem had been oversleeping lately. Since he'd been leaving the dogs out, they were not there to roust him from bed. Also, the fact that he had had no odd jobs for most of the summer contributed to his lethargy. He had awakened slowly and had heavy sleep to battle off. As Clem laid there he grimaced, remembering he had failed to go shopping for food and essentials such as cigarettes and coffee and he pictured the kitchen in its old bachelor barrenness. This meant if he wanted any satisfaction promptly, he would have to dress presentably, get in the pickup and drive the eight miles down to the valley store. It was the presentation part that stumped him this morning. No hot water heater. That meant no clean clothes or hot bath. The sleep made him feel indifferent. Screw it; he'd simply bathe cowboy style and rummage through the hamper. Cold water might spark him this morning.

He began by striking a match. He watched the blue smoke snake up into the room. The smell of sulfur always reminded him of his mother. He lit his last cigarette, sitting there on the edge of the high bed dangling his blue, veiny feet. Through the bedroom window he watched a truck and trailer loaded with hay, barrel down the dirt road. He continued to gaze off and followed the trees and ridges up to Cuerno Verde, or Greenhorn or so it is called by gringos today.

Its Spanish name comes from the great Comanche Chief Tabivo Naritgant who wore a wondrous headdress of bison horns painted green, which is said to have a resemblance to the 12,000-foot bald peak. The Chief was killed in 1779 by a force of 500 soldiers under Spanish Governor Juan Bautista de Anza near the St. Charles River north east of here. The whole area was awash in fantastic lore of wild and courageous characters. Clem liked to think he was part of some colorful history, taming the land and raising feed for horses. He stared while smoke strayed from his nose. Clem noticed he was wringing his feet and looked at their bluishness. "Humph." He grunted.

The bedroom was stark. An Edward Curtis print, *An Oasis in the Badlands,* hung crooked behind the bed. Across the room, on a table, under a lamp lay copies of Zane Grey's *The Drift Fence,* and Kenneth Robert's *Northwest Passage,* both had been read to the point of fraying. Near the bed an end table held his wallet, wristwatch, ashtray, a lamp, an unwound Big Ben alarm clock, an arrowhead and a pottery shard inside a jar. On the floor lay his boots on a large rust colored rag rug.

Looking around the room he took a deep drag, groaned, then slid off the side of the bed and settled on his feet and tried to stand erect. His whole body fought this suggestion and let him know with clicks and pops. He arched his back and just about passed out. This caused him to have a coughing fit which brought up a wad of sputum forcing him to trot to the bathroom sink to spit. With his hands holding the sides of the sink he looked up into the mirror at himself panting out of breath. He shook his head back and forth. He'd made it to the bathroom and tried to put a new spin on not having hot water. "That's how them old boys done it. Here we go," he bemoaned…

After the scrubbing ordeal he managed to find a cleanish shirt, dressed and tried to slip on his boots. One of the leather pull straps gave way causing Clem to keel over on to his side. He held on to the other strap swearing while he rolled to his back now with his foot above him. He fought with the boot refusing to give in. It would not win. His heel finally thumped into place and his legs fell to the floor with such concussion that the room shook, and dust filtered down from ceiling cracks. "How could a morning be so blasted hard," he thought while his breathing settled back to normal. Before he left the room, he peeked into his wallet. There was a twenty, two fives and a one-dollar bill. With a quick calculation he figured he'd make do.

The clomp of his boots was loud coming down the stairs. The house was still, empty and cold. The sun was making its way in from the east windows spilling onto the floor warming the old Navajo rugs. The dogs were lying on the porch in the morning sun and they looked up when Clem opened the screen door. They did not rise to greet him but laid their heads back down and resumed their morning siesta. He clomped along the wooden porch and down the steps toward his truck. The three steps winced and squeaked. "Yeah, yeah, you're next," Clem addressed them with a wave.

His Chevrolet truck was still caked with last winter's mud. The truck's windows were at least clean. The wipers still had decent blades. That's been good enough. Hell, it's just a lease. With a spit he kicked the tire and looked out over the field. His Appaloosa mare swung her tail leisurely and looked up towards Clem. Bits of what she was nibbling on dropped and floated to the ground. It was a sight Clem was momentarily savoring. The old horse trailer was pitched forward near the shed looking lame and despondent in its rusting shades of dereliction. The corral gate banged in the breeze and made a deep bell like sound from deserted foggy harbors. Then a faint squeak and cry came from the hinge. It was a lonely sound. It hung in the dry air and then the breeze slithered through the tall tan grass as if someone was whispering. Clem made a dry spitting sound, the tip of his tongue pressed between his lips then drawn in quickly, allowing a brief burst of air before his lips closed. It was an old oral quirk ingrained from smoking filterless cigarettes which often left a bit of tobacco on the tongue or lips. He kicked the tire, then cocked his hat forward and scratched behind his ear. He returned his gaze to the trailer and read the faded letters across the side. "Clem's Appaloosas." *This is no good,* he thought and reached for his cigarettes that weren't there. The mare bowed her head. The gate again banged and cried.

Clem turned and climbed into the cab, hanging on to his straw hat with one hand and pulling the door shut behind with the other. Clem began to search for a cigarette. First, he looked in the glove box, then on the floor, lastly the ash tray. As he leaned towards the ash tray, he bumped the rearview mirror and sent it out of whack and catawampus. No cigarettes anywhere. He adjusted the mirror and caught a fast glimpse of himself. *Who was that tired old guy with sad eyes,* he thought and quickly looked away. Clem pushed that thought aside and felt relieved that he at least kept the truck in decent running condition. He rallied his pride, silently self acknowledging his prowess of auto mechanics.

As Clem eased the truck along the dirt road the tires made crunching sounds rolling over pebbles and stones. He watched the road in its tans and grays blur by and images came to him… He was standing on the shore of a lake his father had taken him to. It was in the mountains and there was a cabin. The lake had been stocked with trout. He'd been fishing the entire morning but had not had so much as a nibble. Losing interest, he began to pitch stones into the lake. He was in awe of the calm peacefulness of the body of water and its surroundings. The lake was deep, green-blue, and mirror glassy. After a while, with all his might, he skimmed a last stone that bounced ten times, and then was swallowed up by the lake. He stood there, amazed, watching the ripples radiate. He was never any good at throwing or skipping stones but each time the smooth stone glanced off the water he counted and was stunned when he reached ten…

A faint realization hit Clem as if somebody was knocking on his hood. He looked up to see he had passed his turn and was about to careen into a neighbor's driveway. He slammed on the brakes. A plume of road dust billowed behind him as he came to a stop.

"Sons of bitches, I'll be god damned," he growled in wide-eyed shock.

"What's the big idea," he spoke to the empty cab as if there were someone to blame. Just at that moment he remembered he was coming out of a morning day-dreaming stupor and that was the reason he past his turn. While Clem quickly pondered, he picked up a slight but pungent gastric stench. "I must've let one fly," he questioned himself in puzzled denial. "Good god," he mumbled.

As he backed out crossing the skid marks in the road, he looked in his rearview mirror to make sure no one had witnessed his blunder. "God damn! Wake up and pay attention," he scolded himself. Clem wove on down the road as it curved towards the creek. He stopped at the bridge and looked at the stream bubbling and foaming. For a shy moment he was lost in suspended and drawn out seconds. He saw his life compacted into a single drop of rain falling into the Cuerno Verde Creek, mingling and dissolving into life's eons of time. Red and yellow leaves ran the small eddies and currents around the rocks. Stellar Jays dive-bombed insects among the bushes and trees. "There it was again," he blinked and chewed the inside of his upper lip. Clem imitated flicking a cigarette butt and stepped on the accelerator, zinging stones out from under his tires.

As he turned onto Highway 165 on the right along the Greenhorn Creek, the cottonwood trees gave birth to a flock of buzzards. Fifty or more bald craggy creatures radiated in a flapping horde rising as if from a vortex of witch's brew, some phenomena like a hundred-year flood, from a black cloud to thinner and thinner, to specks of pepper blown from the face of the earth. Clem was getting the creeps and felt the goosebumps rise between his shoulder blades. He shivered in the heat. He almost came to a stop but caught a glimpse of cars coming and sped off. From the rearview mirror he could still see the buzzards circling. "The only reason they'd do that is if there's a carcass. The stench of death brings them," he said.

Clem thought he was indifferent to death, but death has become a systematic fact in all its nuances. People were dropping like flies lately. Today Clem was feeling his age and mortality. He hated to go to funerals ever since his mother passed on nearly twenty years earlier. The Grim Reaper kept popping up lately. Ever since he turned sixty "around the corner" was everywhere, friends, family, town folk. Just the other day his neighbor, Shirley Lope, told him about a little boy that committed suicide. The death of this little boy, a stranger, other than the fact that he only lived a mile away, was beyond him. He could not fathom the idea that an 11-year-old would commit suicide by hanging. *What was the world coming to? Where does a kid, that age get an idea of that magnitude and have the wherewithal to carry it out? What kinds of pressures was a young boy subjected to? Maybe they'd have something in the local paper about it*, he thought.

Clem wasn't paying attention to his speed. "Let 'em pass. Screw 'em," he said. The buzzards were still on his mind. "Like the scattering of a dark-feathered union meeting or ancient smoldering funeral pyre spewing up beastly vulture spirits." He kept trying to describe it. He remembered one time a year ago down at the local community church the preacher came up to him. He asked why Clem didn't attend church more often. Clem replied, "It's so darn hot and stuffy there." The preacher retorted with, "It's gonna be a lot hotter and stuffier where you'll be going if you don't." Clem chuckled to himself. He liked that kind of humor. He liked the no-nonsense preacher but still couldn't get himself to go to church on any regular basis. He liked being himself and he felt uncomfortable in the midst of others, who didn't approve of his way of joking, his way of interacting. Clem was rough, uncouth, a filthy sort of bugger, some would say. Clem liked it that way though. He tested people, threw them off guard, watched their reaction to see who could put up with him, accept him on his own terms. "God, I need a cigarette," he coughed.

At the Get 'n Go up ahead on the left, cars were gassing up and a steady stream of morning commuters exited the glass doors with to-go coffees in hand. Clem pulled into the only space available, next to a cop car. He got out and rounded his truck moving to the driver side of the cop. "This must be home, huh?"

Patrolwoman Patsy Evans turns, "Say what?"

Clem pointed to the faded handicap sign, "You're in the right space," he spat and slapped the top of the patrol car.

A large stocky gal with short cropped red hair, Patsy Evans had been the local sheriff for the past five years. The sheriff's sub-station was located just around the corner in Fountain Square. She was easygoing but sharp as a tack.

Just then Glenda Jenkins hobbled up with her bad leg, peered in and shouted at Patsy, "How come you don't haul his ass off." Clem looked up and said, "Here's trouble with blonde hair." The three of them all chuckled at the same time.

"How ya doing Clem?" Glenda said.

"A day late and dollar short. The harder I tries the worse it gets."

"Well nothing's changed." Glenda waved him off with a smile, waved at Patsy and hobbled on past into the store.

Patsy was getting a call on the radio about a man blocking a school bus on a county road up in Rye. Patsy was in a rush. "The shit people pull! Gotta go." She backed out while Clem's hand was still on the hood. Clem stood there, watched her drive off and spat. He mulled over what Glenda had just remarked. *Nothing's changed.* Did she say that off the cuff or am I always a day late and dollar short?

Inside Get 'n Go Clem made a beeline to the coffee dispensers. With a frustrated sigh he began assembling his fix. In the Styrofoam cup he gingerly dumped chemically devised cream, then poured in steaming coffee. The concoction fizzed and swirled as he looked for the lids. Plucking up the first one he saw he worked at snapping it over the flimsy cup. Coffee spurted out over the rim and Clem swore under his breath but was overheard by a woman standing behind him, waiting her turn at the coffee trough. "Now, now. It's a little too early for that, try the next size," she smiled, and he caught it in his half-turn side glance. Clem followed her guidance and daubed up his spill with a napkin and scuttled off for a jar of instant coffee and creamer, a package of Little Debbie Donuts then had to stand in line for cigarettes. At the front of the line was Jean Stanley probably the prettiest unattached woman in the valley. She was stocking up on cigarettes and pop. Clem yelled for her. Jean turned around and acknowledged him by a quick lift of her chin. She paid and was making her way out when Clem again yelled, "If I had a swing like that in my backyard, I'd put a fence around it." With that, most of the men in the store now had turned and were looking directly at the blushing woman. Jean turned as she was exiting the glass doors and gave Clem a less then friendly grin.

Finally, at the head of the line Clem asked for a carton of Marlboro 100s red hard packs. He paid for his items and the cashier bagged the goods and handed him his change. Almost forgetting to ask for a batch of matches, he pirouetted on one foot and requested them all at once. The cashier threw the handful of matches in the bag then she looked at him saying, "You really know how to charm the gals!" Before he could respond she was cashing out the next customer in line. Clem gently moved along in the customer flow headed for the exit.

Outside Clem began to feel the first sensations of coffee deprivation at the base of his skull. "A day and a half without joe and this is the price," he said while digging into the bag for his cigarettes. He stopped at the front of his truck, placed the Styrofoam cup on the hood, fumbled with the carton, stripped the cellophane and started tapping the pack against his palm. He filched a cigarette and lit it in one motion while looking at the morning crowd. *I just love the smell of Marlboros and sulfur*, he thought. His head was gradually aching more. He popped the lid off the coffee and sipped. Grimacing at bitter hotness he began thinking of his coffee and cigarette habit.

*Just how long have I been smoking? Off and on almost thirty-five years? Yeah mostly on. Well, we all gotta die of something, so it might as well be something you like. Ah hell, my Dad smoked for forty years and lived to eighty. Small pleasure. Yeah that's all I got is small pleasures.*

The hood was warm from the engine, so Clem leaned there in the parking lot smoking, sipping, waiting and watching.

Clem was jolted to reality by a kick to his rear. Coffee spilt and ran every which-a-way.

"I thought someone should kick your ass, you dirty old man," Jean said.

"Well I'll be god-damned you scared the shit out of me," Clem huffed.

"I hope I didn't get any on me," said Jean inspecting her boot. "Ain't you got anything better to do than harassing women in this town?"

"Shit, I wasn't harassing you, I was just overcome by the obvious," Clem spilled.

"Well maybe next time let the obvious stand on its own or I'll have to really kick your ass," she said while pulling a pack of cigarettes out of her purse, extracting one and lighting it.

"You kick me three ways to hell if you like," Clem laughed. He took a puff then said, "I saw your boy friend."

"What boyfriend?"

"That burly young stud at the hardware store."

"Dan?"

"I don't know," Clem said.

"You bastard, you're fishing?"

Clem spit and chuckled, "I hear you're in love."

"You are a work of art! Shit, you don't know nothing," Jean chuckled back. "How 'bout those Broncos?"

"Broncos my ass, did you see that Cowboys game?"

They both took turns taking drags from their respective cigarettes.

"You still got that Stihl chain saw for sale?"

"Yep, it's collecting dust in the shed and probably needs fresh fuel. Why? You want to buy it?"

"No, my brother wants an extra when he goes for wood next week. He's tired of driving all the way up to Sheep Mountain and having that old Craftsman crap out on him."

"The saw's in good shape. I'll dust 'er off, tune 'er up and look 'er over. It's a good saw," boasted Clem. He walked over to his truck and found a pencil and paper and scribbled his number down, came back and handed it to Jean. "Have him call me."

"What are you asking?"

"I'd like to get two hundred. It's a champ of a saw. Have 'im call and we'll haggle'"

Jean took the paper, "I'll give him the number. Thanks."

They both threw their butts on the ground and didn't bother to twist them out, just left them there to smolder on the oil-soaked parking lot.

"See ya later," Jean said and turned to leave.

"See ya gorgeous. I'll tell your boyfriend that I saw ya," Clem yelled back.

Jean flipped him off without turning around and got in her big ol' red Chevy truck. *Not many women can fit a truck cab without looking butch*, he thought.

Clem watched her back out and drive onto 165. He shook his head from side to side and said to himself, "That woman is built." He wasn't interested in her per se but he could still appreciate a well crafted woman. After all he *was* still above ground.

Clem groped his shirt pockets and found his cigarettes and lit one and gave womenfolk some more thought. All and all he believed women to be sheer trouble. His divorce had left him bitter. But that never kept him from looking. From the time he was a teenager he'd swore the actress Gene Tierney was the most seductive woman he'd ever seen on the wide screen or in real life. Her seductively innocent overbite gnawed at his loins. He used Gene as a standard bar for comparison. Not many came up to par. Although a realist and knowing he was no suave and debonair catch himself, he thought his first wife "a looker," his second, even better. He smiled and spit.

Rainey, or as she was known then, Rayann Timberly, had always been a breath of clear air. They had met during the period when Clem first got the wild hair to breed horses and he was on a mission, visiting various horse ranches in northern

New Mexico. He was searching, probing, exploring the idea but mainly decompressing from a nasty divorce. It was an autumn night near twenty-five years ago and he was hold up in one of those roadside motels near the Plaza in Las Vegas. He'd stepped out and was wandering the Plaza feeling lost and winded but too restless to stay put at the motel.

The magnets of destiny were pulling, so he walked. Walking helped. He could think and figure better at a walking pace. He met her at one of those old-time movie theater ticket booths along the rippled sidewalk. As he walked past the glass booth, he felt something similar to when his shirt had gotten snagged on barbed wire and he slowed dramatically to try to not rip it. He stopped and stood there staring at her through the glass. He saw his reflection and her face behind the glass partition melding together. Her short upper lip left her front teeth beckoning him.

She asked if he wanted a ticket and he made up some cock 'n bull about wanting one of the movie posters 'cause he collected them. She told him that the owner was going to change them out tonight and to come back around midnight when she got off and she'd probably have one for him. She added, as he was about to turn, that there was a carnival in the park, and it was the last night. They could go to it if he was interested. He did come back, and they wandered the warm fall sidewalks in the carnival night. That's how it happened. That's how it always happens.

Clem blinked then looked at his cigarette. It was half ash and about to drop. His daydreams were eating up the morning. Clem's stomach growled and his head pounded. On highway 165 several vehicles drove by in a line. "Look at all them damn cars," Clem mumbled. Back when he moved here in the mid-seventies, cars were a scarcity. People waved at one another or lifted a finger off the steering wheel acknowledging neighbor to neighbor, little courtesies of a small town. Now it seemed to him that the big city dwellers had invaded. They drive too fast, tailgate all the way up and down the mountain. He laughed thinking how many get their comeuppance hitting deer or sliding off the road. He saw them all the time with one hand on the steering wheel and the other holding a cell phone. "Damn fools," he spit and cocked his straw hat. It was getting late.

Clem yanked himself into the driver's seat slavishly trying to decide whether to grocery shop or not. He grabbed the Little Debbie's fumbling with the cellophane. They broke open and powdered him in his haste. He stuffed one in his mouth and brushed the white dust from his wranglers, almost gagging but recovering with a dry swallow. He would shop but just for necessities: dog food, eggs, bread, peanut butter, potatoes and toilet paper. He'd get by and eat less.

The market was empty, thank God. He made fast work of it holding all the items in his arms at the checkout counter. He paid and grumbled at the price of food. The checkout lady smiled back saying

"Ain't it the pits?" with a wave of the receipt. Clem shuffled to the automatic doors with the plastic bag of groceries lollygagging at his side. As the sliding doors parted, the days aroma wrapped around Clem's face like a wanton genie with the tempting invitation of a wish. His urges tumbled and twisted in his gut like way too much old coffee grinds. Little sweat beads popped at his temples and his ears rang. He made believe he remembered those urges, yearning for the safety of the truck's cab. The air was filled with past lives and hung-out-to-dry memories in suffocating proximity. "God damn I need caffeine," Clem sweated. As he was about to step up into the cab, he remembered he had forgotten a paper. He heaved the groceries onto the front floorboard, turned back towards the market, feeling for change in his front hip pocket.

He fed the quarters into the newspaper dispenser, grabbed a paper and let the lid clang shut. Scanning the headlines as he walked drops of sweat fell from his forehead onto the paper. He glanced up to the blaze of sun, did his little tongue-lip dry spit tick and clambered back into the truck.

The newspaper was devoid of any mention of the hanging. Clem was overtly curious about the "why," as if the paper or family would choose to reveal that tidbit. In any event he once more scanned each page. Nothing, just Middle East problems and fires up and down the front range. He was satisfied and unsatisfied at the same time. On one hand his voyeurism was pulling him in as he was confounded by why a young boy would carry out an act that would have such ramification for himself and his family, and on the other, he did not want to know about the darkness, and could leave it at that. The finality of it caused him to shudder. He took a deep breath and let it out as a slight hiss. His ears were ringing still and he felt a trickle drop from his temple. He watched it soak and spread into the newspaper. In caffeine desperation, he flipped the ignition and escaped from the parking lot.

There was no sense in going home. He wanted diversion. So, he turned left instead of right on 165 chugging towards Max's. He could rustle up coffee and conversation there and ponder more immediate problems.

Max's was a poor substitute for the closed-and-forgotten Mary Lou's. Mary Lou's used to be across the interstate in a gas station turned café, a cramped, greasy-spoon affair that packed them in, open for breakfast and lunch only. Mary Lou knew what ranchers wanted. Coffee that kept coming and meals that left you looking for a new belt buckle hole. Folks didn't mind waiting for a seat and on occasion even sashayed up to a table not yet cleared, a familiarity without the contempt. But that was then, and Max's was now. Clem smirked to himself as he cranked the wheel into the half-full parking lot. The man who now owned the place was named Bill, not Max. "Some newfangled marketing ploy," he fittingly mumbled.

Clem was greeted with, "Look what the cat dragged in," as he pushed through the stained-glass doors.

"Hey, I'm just what you're looking for," he quipped.

"And what would that be?" retorted the register girl.

"A paying customer."

"Touché."

They both mock-laughed.

"Sit anywhere," she said, "but be nice."

"Ah… you take all the fun out of it."

"Coffee or are you just here to look?" she asked over her shoulder.

"Both."

"I'll send Dotty by with a mug and a pair of glasses."

"I'll be waitin', darlin'."

Clem shook hands with several curmudgeon types like himself, receiving advice on his grooming and morning outfit. In return he grimaced passable responses then disengaged. He found a table by the far end of the room next to the window. He nestled in as well as he could fidgetting with thick fingers trying to find his way without a coffee mug. He instinctively groped his front shirt pocket for the hard pack then thought better. The world had changed. Smoking had become an affront to civilized man. He was grouchy and critical and seriously jonesing for coffee. He saw the buzzards circling in his mind, the noose taut and the skin stretching. The pit of his stomach tightened. His eyes wandered out the window, across the interstate to an escarpment in the distance. The hubbub of the café faded as he meandered in the reverie of his thoughts… *it was*

*Ferguson's horse ranch south of Walsenburg. He was riding a young Appaloosa. His favorite Stetson hat cocked in the sun. A warm laughter ran to him from behind as Rainey called to wait. She was on an old dappled gray mare. She wanted to trade mounts. She wanted to ride the new horse, the first one they would buy together...*

"Black and beautiful," Dotty barked at the same time handing Clem a menu. "What'll it be, hon?"

With one hand holding the menu, Clem turned and looked at the mug with its beautiful streams of steam lilting above the white porcelain mouth. With the deftness of a rattler, he struck the handle with an instinctive finger lifting it to his lips.

"*Some*body's hurtin'."

"You are my newest, best friend."

"Stand in line, sweetie. It's only 8:30."

"It seems like forever." Clem's gulps turned to stifled sips as he regained some sense of calm.

"The herd is about to stampede hon. You doing the regular, or dieting today?"

"Besides this coffee, you're the next best thing I've seen. Why don't you fix me up with your sister, the cinnamon roll and leave the pot?"

"Ooh, you *do* know how to hurt a girl. One hot bun coming up." Dotty refilled Clem's mug grabbed the menu from his hand and turned on a dime.

Clem returned to his mug selfishly wishing all women could be like Dotty. The dark liquid rippled inside and reflected the ceiling fan as his hand shook. He caressed it lovingly, sipping in ecstasy. He was conscious of his momentary detachment. He tried to appear normal. He pushed his old stained Stetson off his forehead with one finger. He envisioned Paul Newman as Hud, inspecting the dead cattle in the movie. He returned to the window again, on his Appaloosa, near the escarpment...He sipped. His hand steadied. His memories pinged around in a pinball cluster burst. Clem shut his eyes and gripped the mug tight. He let out a sigh without ever inhaling, letting on the appearance of complete satisfaction with his coffee. "I can do this," he mentally repeated.

"You unsociable codger. You look like a sick cur. Whose funeral you been to?" Marvin Reesebalm, owner of the valleys only trash service, bellowed.

"Yours if you're not careful. Don't you know better than to sneak up on a feeding dog? How ya doin?" Clem reached across the table to shake the man's hand, smiling, not letting go of his mug or rising.

"Me and my boys over there," he gestured to a table by the stained-glass doors. Clem waved. "Headed for LaVeta to cut wood. Wanna join us?"

"No thanks. Think I'll stick around the house and saw my own logs." Both men chuckled in their manliness, eyes sparkling in knowing.

"We could use an old hand on a Stihl. The cooler's filled with Buckhorn and deviled-ham sandwiches.

"What the hell you cuttin' wood this early for?"

"Gonna learn these boys a thing or two about hard work."

"Well don't let a trunk fall on 'em."

"You sure I can't drag your lazy ass off this mountain?"

"Mighty tempting, but I got a truck load of chores to tend to and a water heater that's gone kablooey."

"And a mountain of logs to saw. You ain't getting any better at lying." They again shook hands and gleamed at one another. "You have another cup now, you look like you need it," said Marvin before he moved on.

Dotty was back, filled the mug like a calf on a tit and gone like a fly on a draft, all the while Clem still clutched his porcelain heaven. His at-ease unfurled and finally came to terms in his element. His MO of traipsing around town, annoying people with his caustic humor, his sarcastic banter and love of double-entendre, kept tabs on what's what. The bustle of the clattering camaraderie of jokes and jests fueled his social animal. His animal had suffered and now was soothed in Dotty's luxurious black liquid.

Clem's gaze into the mug lingered. He watched the slight reflection of the ceiling fan and the circular ripples undulating from the center. After a moment it dawned on him that his leg was bouncing under the table, and that was causing the ripples. He placed a hand on his knee consciously stopping the incessant bounce. He returned to the mug and sipped. He listened to the conversation from the next table. The men gabbed about fires flaring up and down the Front Range all summer and they agreed, "We'll get our due, sooner or later." Shutting his eyes, he began to drift. Drifting... floating... soft... smooth... *he saw Rainey. They were at a quarry. The water was deep and dark. They were standing on the shoreline up to their ankles both of them wiggling their toes and grabbing the gravel, feeling it rub and scratch their toes. Their hands touched and their fingers wove in and out of each other. Their toes carried the conversation and their lips were useless. The moment's description could not be uttered other than to silently enjoy. A spring sun ricocheted off the water's surface lighting up their bodies. He looked at her and the scintillating beads of perspiration forming on her temples. He started to reach for her...*

"Hon?...Here we go! Hot buns you don't want to miss. Anyone there?" Dotty jived in a professional impatience.

Clem was lost. Clem was engrossed. And part of Clem didn't want to come back.

"Huh? What? Who? Yeah!" He jerked back dribbling the coffee on to his paper napkin.

"Don't fret, hon, I'll get it." Putting the cinnamon roll square in front of Clem and grabbing the napkin, wiping, all in a single motion. She buzzed off as the ringing sound of the fork settled on the formica table. Clem, still in the quasi-haze, blinking, holding the coffee mug now stared at the cinnamon rings and white globs of glaze. He felt nauseous. He felt his heart fall silent. He tried to hush his thoughts, hide his visions. Both legs were bouncing now. Something was encroaching, approaching him, ever closer. It moved in, coiling, suffocating dangerously, a hum. Clem's ears were ringing and then all at once the crash of jabbering hammered down on him with the embarrassment of reality. The roar of voices exploded. His eyes widened. He held his breath. He blinked at the pounding in his chest. As he breathed, each breath became clearer. The voices of the cafe, from each table, each person, became audible. It was only voices, patrons talking, laughing, and eating. Clem was stunned.

"Shit!" he buried the word in a hissing sigh as if blowing on the hot mug of coffee. He sipped it and picked up the fork. He concentrated on the task of eating the cinnamon roll. Edging a morsel with the fork he lifted it to his mouth and chewed. With eyes closed he relished the temporary escape from phantoms. He chewed, surprised at the gushing saliva reaction to the sweetness of the sugary glaze. That was it. He was only in need of sustenance. Maybe his blood sugar level was low.

Clem swallowed and opened his eyes. His hand with the fork had already returned to edging another piece of roll and was on a return trip to the mouth. He felt he was an observer to someone else eating. The hand, independent, foreign, aged and blemished, was working away. He fell into its control and opened his mouth repeatedly, finishing the roll.

Dotty appeared and with a single swoop took away the plate and tried to refill Clem's cup, but Clem quickly covered the mug with his palm fearing the headache of caffeine saturation. Dotty spun off, "Be right back with the check, sweetie."

Clem looked at his hand again while he unconsciously cleaned his teeth with his tongue. He pinched a napkin from the table dispenser and wiped his brow, forehead, then mouth in an S curve, finally crumbling the napkin, placing it on the formica tabletop. He placed both hands on his knees and watched the napkin slowly uncrumple. He did not hear Dotty's return with the check or her comment. He was only aware of the slowness of the expanding napkin, the unfolding of hundreds of wrinkles. In the quiet whiteness he reached out and touched Rainey's cheek with the back of a forefinger. Time was glacier, rendered in anti-time. The touch had fragrance and Panavision color and the more he thought the more he missed of what once was.

# Two

Clem found himself back in the truck trying to untangle himself from the clinging fragrance and vivid hues of the ever-persistent "Rainey daydream." Clem patted his pockets for the keys and panicked. He retraced his thoughts and could not think. He kept thinking where, where, in jumbled thinking patterns. He did not know why he was thinking. Rainey was there, the wonderful scent of her there, lavender, rose and sage. The sensation of light was there, yellow, vermilion and tangerine. As he came out of the trance he stared at the keys in the ignition, numbed.

Clem hardly acknowledged the reappearance of the lost keys. In an automaton gesture his hand turned the key, the engine rumbled and he backed up slowly in arthritic fashion. The run of morning commuters had slackened, and the highway was clear.

The view of Cuerno Verde, ten miles on the other side of the valley, brought some sense of relief. As always, the familiar was soothing. Clem tried to breathe consciously.

After a few miles Clem approached Lake Beckwith and decided to turn off. He pulled in under several cottonwood trees and parked. Filching a cigarette from his shirt pocket he lit it and rolled down the window. Clem let his eyes wander from shore, to morning walkers, to fields across the lake, to the gate valves of the Hicklin Ditch. He watched a murder of crows cross the lake and their shadows flicker and skip on the water's surface. Then his eyes went to the cylindrical concrete tower near the spillway that indicated water level marks. He saw Canadian geese float in packs near the marsh. Then something caught his eye. Clem squinted and peered out the front windshield leaning slightly forward. There perched in a distant cottonwood tree was a bald eagle.

"Well I'll be damned." Then he softly whistled, ending it with his dry-lipped spit sound. The air in the cab was still. The smoke from his cigarette barely moved. It hung aloft in variant streaks of gray. Clem watched the eagle move its protruding yellow beak from side to side as it surveyed the surrounding waters.

"Now that's a sight." Clem spoke to himself and then nodded in agreement. As he nodded his sister, Gail, entered his thoughts. Why of all people and now of all times? Maybe the birds. His fall from grace, in Gail's estimation, began with the death of two small finches. She went away on a short trip and he was given charge of the creatures. All was satisfactory until the final two days before her return. The tiny puffs of down were lifeless at the bottom of the cage. He had fed and watered as instructed and yet they perished. He was dumbfounded. He put the birds in the freezer to present as evidence. The incident did not go over well. His sister was visibly shaken and saddened by, in her mind, the tragic blunder of her younger brother.

To Clem it was a simple matter of natural attrition of captive animals that had no business being incarcerated in the first place. Pets come and go, an obvious fact, and Clem gave it little concern, but as a result his relationship with his sister gradually fell stagnant. There were other incidences too and all came to a head one Christmas when she read him the riot act and swore never to have anything to do with him again. As it turned out, it *was* Clem's blunder. He went over it hundreds of times in his head and figured he'd misread the amount of seeds that were in the food dish. What had appeared to be seed was in fact the shell casings left over from the birds splitting the seeds while feeding.

Time's erosion of memory seemed to be of no avail, his sister was lost in its dust. He questioned the bonds of family, the valiant ties of siblings. Just because you are born into a family doesn't necessitate permanent and problem-free interaction. The unforeseen can occur and some people are just plain weird. Gail was weird, not so much in a negative way as she was peculiarly weird in startling ways . . . a free spirit with a sharp and acute mind . . . never a worry in the world for money. But on the other hand, she could always be counted on to forget the teapot on the stove and leave it to melt, and she was constantly late for appointments or important engagements. During conversations she would share amazing information that she would never be suspected of knowing and then not know what day it was. Maybe it was nothing more then quirky behavior and hadn't he himself been acting quirky lately?

Still he gazed at the eagle in a patriotic stupor. "Just 'bout killed 'em off," he mumbled and took a drag on his ash laden cigarette. The ash dislodged falling silently to his thigh. Clem looked at it and rubbed it into his pants. He flicked the cigarette butt out the window and saw it land in the dirt and smolder.

*The women in my life are riding shotgun this morning*, he gravely thought. His Mother, Rainey, and now Gail. Sorcerers with poisonous memory-mists infusing the air, that was what autumn held, rankling one's thoughts and feelings, longing for the past, diluted by longing, distorted by time and infected with unfulfilled wishful desires. Dreams persist and kaleidoscope into tandem dreams that end in the morning sickness that is unexplained other than a scent that lingers the daylong.

Clem looked at wisps of clouds lining the top of Cuerno Verde. A sensation of unbridled quiet invaded the cab. The clouds dissolved and reformed. A sudden shadow broke the moment.

Clem blinked dryly. With a turn of his head he saw where the eagle had been. He turned again to see the eagle glide off into the valley, south towards old Kenny Pounds Road. He continued to watch the bird disappear feeling envious. He returned to the clouds and their misty undulations. Playfully Clem entertained a childlike fantasy that the spirit of Chief Tabivo Naritgant had sent the eagle on a quest to help Clem with a vision. Clem now pondered the possible vision. Was it freedom? Was it power? Was it wisdom? Was it knowledge? Was it understanding? Was it the resignation of all those.

Clem thought of the warrior Naritgant and the battles fought by this brave courageous Comanche leader, this man fraught with purpose. Clem knew he was nothing like the warrior chief. His battles were miniscule, consisting of divorces and working to maintain the meager money flow. His battle with insecurity, he reasoned, was not exactly a battle but more a maintenance issue. He hadn't won but dealt with it on a daily basis. Maybe his lack of confidence was inexorably wrapped up in the stains of his Catholic upbringing. Born a sinner is a tough stain to remove. Although for years now he had touted the phrase "Recovering Catholic" and no longer gave credence to preordained damnation or blame. Still the tendrils of fear and guilt reached out and Clem had been feeling their faint brush. Both broad and fine strokes had been filling life's canvas this morning. In Clem's mind the painting looked a bit dismal. Not a pastoral scene but some abstract expressionist gobbledygook that he'd been plodding through.

Once again Clem looked up at the mountain mist trying desperately to dispel his turbid thoughts. The eagle was gone but the image of white and black spun in his mind, nuns with pointers and yardsticks, the nuns' habits with knife-edged towering wimples. Dominance and rosary beads flowed with heavy ebony crosses. He remembered the humiliation, the deflating of his youthful vigor by stern looks and embarrassing swats. Ear pulling and dunce caps failed to curb young Clem's vibrant energy. He hated and despised those tyrants. He knew why he was a deplorable student. He could not concentrate because he was so easily distracted and nuns honed-in on what they termed "daydreamers." They should have let him run around the block a few times. Consequently, he did poorly in grade school and had ever since been plagued by it with an inferiority complex. Maybe it was not that severe, but he had had bouts of insecurity and worried with doubts throughout his life. He knew more about discipline than how to spell and had been trying to catch up ever since.

The eagle and the nuns migrated to the back of Clem's head. "To hell with eagles and nuns," he spit through his teeth. He had prevailed. He was sixty-five and retired living on a small allotment of Social Security benefits along with odd jobs. But it was difficult to forget his past. Wasn't it what created his present? Wasn't it what influenced his future? He was exhausted and in a quandary whether he wanted to deal with all his past this morning.

Clem swallowed dryly and patted his breast pocket for another cigarette. The mist on the mountain had vanished and now the cab was stifling in the morning sun. Clem let the cigarette dangle from his lips as he clutched the truck into gear. He was perturbed by his anger. The tires spun in the dirt then caught solid ground jarring the truck.

From Cuerno Verde Road Clem veered left onto Blanco Street stopping at the intersection of Highway 165. He looked both ways and had to wait for oncoming traffic. Huge self-contained campers rumbled by. "Tourists! Good riddance!" He squintched his nose and rubbed it with a forearm sleeve.

On entering the highway, he sped up. Being back on the move felt better. A mile or so up, Clem passed a building on his right across from Beverly Place. There he had seen a cougar in two leaps bound across the highway back some thirty years ago. Also, he remembered many fun evenings at the Sanchez's Mexican Restaurant known by all the locals as "Taco Rock." As far as dives went, it was one of his favorites. Beer and a combo plate for under five bucks. The booths were horribly uncomfortable, but the beer was cold, and servings were plentiful, tasty and hot. It was gone now replaced by some real estate outfit. He missed the place. He missed a lot of things. *Change is a pain in the ass*, Clem silently pouted. He thought of the saying, "The only things you can count on are taxes and death." He wanted to add "change" to that adage and did so slowly repeating the word "change" several times. For a brief instant he considered a change for himself. Maybe it would be good, but change to what? That was the stumper. He was settled. He was getting by, comfortable if he paid attention. The thing was that he was not paying attention. He was becoming lazy and complacent. He smoked too much. He was living on the outside of his life, going along for the tour, looking down at it as if he were simply a passenger on a carnival ride. He knew he spent too much time "shooting the shit" with anyone he met. He could manage to dispense with an entire day in that behavior and had been doing it more and more. "Change might be the thing," he nodded tapping repeatedly on the steering wheel.

Clem gave a sudden laugh. The idea of change began to piss him off. It wasn't that you simply went out and painted your house or bought a new truck. He knew it was much more. He would have to work towards personal growth. Find new interests. Make an effort and set a goal. This was all fine and dandy, but by god it was hard enough just keeping up with the wear and tear of day after day. Repairing this or fixing that, it was never ending. He knew he should buckle down and get to work, stop piddling away the rest of his life. Yes, he knew it . . .

Clem looked up from the valley road gliding along its feminine curves and undulations that outlined the Greenhorn Creek, an artery of the mountains water shed that bled year-round. He'd fished in that creek and gutted lots of brook trout. He'd slipped on her mossy rock and sipped her gelid waters. He'd watched snakes snatch minnows and heard her murmurs and gulps. He had had an intimacy with her. And now a million years of sculpturing whittled down to a picture postcard moment in glances from the cab's window. Snowstorms, rainstorms, drought and flood inch by inch the grandeur of the valley emerged. There were still sections along the creek that hadn't changed course for eons. The rock formations etched by water have only deepened and become more severe. Clem likened these to be Mother Earth's smiling wrinkles. He accepted these small rationalizations to the aging process on the grounds that mother earth needed all the help she could get. After all, mankind has trampled and torn into her mercilessly and he knew he was part of the infestation that contributed to her blemished complexion. All women should be afforded the compliment. To his way of thinking, this gal was infinitely more lovely with age.

There it was again. "I got gals on my mind," Clem mused and then began to sing in a drawl with an obnoxious country twang. He got through the phrase once then stopped croaking. He sure as shit was no singer.

All of a sudden Clem was fidgety. He realized that he'd been wiggling the cigarette between his teeth. He'd forgotten all about it and hadn't lit it yet. He pulled it from his lips and looked at it puzzled. "Now that's a first," he said. Clem continued along the highway holding the steering wheel with the cigarette between his fingers. He did his tongue-lip-spit noise several times, shaking his head from side to side, alternating looks from the road to the cigarette.

The highway was calmer now. Most of the traffic was well on its way to Pueblo, Walsenburg or the Springs. The bedroom community had emptied out and deposited most of its townsfolk at various jobs. Clem watched the white lines dart by. He looked up at the foothills rising from the valley. He could see the scrub oak with its tinge of red beginning. The massive mountain grew even larger as he approached it. Turning the bend at the Credit Union, sun-drenched fields and cow pastures opened up. The steeples from the Catholic and Methodist churches and the Mormon Temple came into view. Rattlesnake Hill jutted out above the small town of Rye. He could see the skeleton of the old Christmas star hanging from its rocks. He had to admit again it had a postcard feel to it. Sort of unreal, like the feeling tourists get on first sight, he imagined.

A breeze from the cab's open window gave Clem a refreshing reprieve from the morning's torment. Maybe change was inevitable for him. The fresh air stirred his choices. Clem turn left into the Post Office lot, parked, and walked to the entrance. Hitting the automatic door switch while wiggling the unlit cigarette in his bite, he strolled in. He could hear the ladies behind the wall of mailboxes gabbing away as they sorted mail. He inserted the mail key and opened the box. It was stuffed. Clem worked at the tight wad of junk mail finally freeing it only to drop most of it as it left the box. He hissed a curse between his teeth still clamped on the filter of the cigarette. He fumbled and picked at the droppings. He hoped the ladies behind the wall couldn't hear him grunt as he squatted there on the floor.

After all was gathered, he plopped the bundle on a table next to a trash can and began to chuck most of it. When the sorting was done there remained only three bills: electric, telephone and another overdue lease payment for his truck. "Blood suckers," he garbled, with the cigarette still between his teeth, then exited.

Seated in the cab, Clem placed his mail on the dashboard and pushed in the dash lighter. He waited in silence. He could hear tiny whistles from his nose hairs as he breathed. The lighter popped. Clem flinched a bit. He yanked it out and gingerly stuck it to the end of his cigarette and sucked. While returning the lighter he exhaled a billow of smoke, thinking something was wrong. The smell was different. No sulfur. That lingering scent of mother's memory was missing.

As the truck entered the driveway Clem swerved to avoid his blue heelers that had rushed out to meet him. As he opened the door, both jumped in the cab wagging their tail stumps. He quickly flicked his cigarette butt in the dirt and started scratching and petting the dogs. They were everywhere at once licking him and sniffing the grocery bag containing the dog food. "You only love me when you're hungry," he spoke to them. Both cocked their heads with ears perked at the word "hungry", then got even more excited. He shooshed them out of the cab and gathered the grocery bags.

Clem walked up the few steps as the dogs nipped at his heels and each other, yipping and dancing playfully. He put the bags on a porch chair next to the front door and patted his pocket for keys. "Damn" he said and turned, being nipped all the way back to the cab. He reached in, pulled the keys out of the ignition and once more started for the house. "Get," he shouted at the dogs. They ran past and stood at the front door, stumps wiggling, and waited.

The kitchen felt cool as Clem placed the bags on the breakfast table. He wiped his forehead with his forearm sleeve and grabbed the bag with dried kibble. The dogs were at their bowls almost pushing them toward him. Their animated tongues mimicked their rapid breaths. They watched their master approach with the food. "Get," he growled. The dogs backed off while Clem filled the bowls and slid them apart with his foot. As he walked away the dogs were on the bowls instantly.

Clem carried the dog food into the pantry and dropped it on the floor in the corner. He put the potatoes and bread on top of the refrigerator. The carton of eggs was slightly crushed so he opened it to check. The dogs in their hullabaloo had inadvertently broken two of the eggs. He walked over to the feeding dogs and stood above the bowls. "Get," he said and scooped out the damaged eggs equally into each of the bowls. He then placed the carton on a shelf in the refrigerator and rinsed his hands at the sink.

Over the years Clem had become rather conservative in his finances. Well to be honest he had downright budgeted himself into a tightwad. Over time it got easier to not spend money. Then it just settled in like winter and he got used to it. He did not consider himself poor, but who does? "An economical son-of-a-bitch" is how he referred to himself. Outsiders had a different name. He'd worked for lots of rich folks, so he knew he was not rich. But out of self-pride or denial, he silently and successfully convinced himself he was not poor. He held tight to his veneer of dignity.

The kitchen was quiet other than the final lapping noise and scooting of bowls from the dogs. Clem dried his hands on a towel hanging from the refrigerator, returned it and straightened it neatly. He touched the handle then slid his hand across the surface of the refrigerator. He lipped the word *icebox* and thought, *Mom always called it "icebox."* He had called it *icebox* all his life until he and Rainey got hitched. She insisted he stop. It bugged her. He understood and complied. She was younger and he wanted it to work. He didn't want to make the same mistakes again. After all it was a small concession in her mind but a lifetime habit in his. Occasionally the word slipped out and she would say "what" and he would say "oops" and life would go on.

The package of toilet paper remained on the table. He grabbed it as he walked by, split the plastic casing with a thumbnail and put two rolls in the bathroom just off the kitchen. He then carried the other two upstairs for the bedroom bathroom.

He replaced the empty roll, urinated and flushed. Then he walked back downstairs. The dogs were now settled by the front door cleaning themselves in satisfaction. They looked up at him. Their ears then went erect and both jumped to attention. They started whimpering and then began to howl and made for the door. Clem look puzzled and then a far-off rumble began. It happened quickly, so quickly one was taken by surprise. Clem actually ducked and the ear-shattering roar filled the room. The house trembled. Clem covered his ears and was screaming "god damn" as he went to the front living-room window. He pushed the curtain aside and looked out. The cadence had lessened, and the dogs were barking, scratching at the baseboard. It was a military fly-over. They happen infrequently but were terrifying. Clem opened the door letting the dogs rush out, barking. He stepped onto the porch, held a post with one hand and looked up in the sky, shielding the sun from his eyes with the other. He spotted a tiny gray object just going out of sight over Cuerno Verde peak to the south. Another terrible roar began, and he saw the dogs go crazy and felt the porch tremble. He covered his ears, a jet fighter on training runs from the Air Force Academy out of Colorado Springs. This southern portion of the Front Range air space was a designated corridor for mission training flights. He remembered the meetings held at the Rye High School auditorium a few years ago. There were plenty of objections, but the meeting was only symbolic. The flyovers and surrounding communities would have to co-exist.

The second roar had subsided, and a faint rumble took its place. The dogs ran back to the porch and jumped at Clem's legs. He batted them away and looked up at the translucent jet stream left behind. Crows were cawing in the pines across the road. Other dogs were baying from distant houses. The yellow field regained its composure and the sound of a breeze was felt rather than heard. Several red-winged black birds flew to power lines above the porch, clutching the wire and clicking in an annoying grievance.

It was not only disturbing to be shocked by the ungodly sound, but it reminded Clem of the continuing war in the Middle East, which he found depressing. The U.S. presences in Iraq and Afghanistan and the turmoil resulting from 9/11 . . . you could forget all of it living out here in the mountains, isolated. "A can of worms, a can of worms," Clem repeated and shook his head bending over to calm the dogs. "Life is nasty, brutish, and short," he spoke to them but couldn't remember who said it. The dogs looked up, one blue eye each.

A quiet settled over the field and mountainside, the kind that induces thoughts. An instinctual "all clear" was sounded for the unfettered dogs to sprawl on the warm porch. Clem's stomach growled. He was thinking of Rainey again and a poem she once wrote. ". . . *Time is an illusionist, one day in shimmering youth it is eternal and one day in graying age it is infinitesimal. Life is a flight into its invisible arms, and we are each caressed and crushed in its surrendering love.*" His stomach growled. In his mind he mulled it over and countered with, "Time is a racehorse named *Whoa*." He spit in the weeds, stepped off the porch, looked down and kicked the dirt. He shoved his hands in his back pants pockets and stood there. These were candy-coated memories. He was cherry-picking the best-of-the-best in his thoughts of her. Maybe the mind salvages the good thoughts and sparingly doles them out in troubled times. If so, he didn't mind. It was much more soothing to think about Rainey than military jets preparing for combat. He rocked back and forth on his heels just staring at the dirt.

There was a crinkling sound and Clem raised his head. It was Jacob Dresden pedaling up Greenhorn Road on his mountain bike. Clem watched him ponderously approach.

"That's a hell of a climb," Clem waited.

Jacob leaned off the bike, panting and came to a rest just in front of Clem's yard and yelled, "It wouldn't be so bad if it wasn't so hot."

Clem walked towards the property gate. "What are you doing up here, you lost?"

"I needed some exercise. My back gets sore driving the school bus."

"Are you off today?"

"Nah, just between routes."

"Damned hot."

"Yeah, d'you hear that jet?"

"Shit, that'd make a cow have a stillborn."

"Well it sure freaked me out."

"Them dogs there went plum berserk."

"I'll bet."

Clem spat, then filched a cigarette from his pack and stuck it in his mouth. Tried different pockets and found his matches, ripped one off and struck it. You couldn't see the flame in the sun, but the sulfur smoke hovered in a blue moment. "Where'd you steal that bike?"

Jacob ignored the jibe and answered. "When are you gonna cut these weeds, you might be able to see the house."

Clem liked that. He liked this kid. A rock'n roller from the City of Angels.

"Hey, you know why Mexico doesn't have submarines?"

"What, is this a joke?"

"Yeah."

"Beats me."

"'Cause adobe dissolves in water." Clem snickered through his nose. "You know why Mexicans don't have Bar-B-Que's?"

"Because beans fall through the grill. Yeah, I heard that one.

They both smiled slightly.

"Well, look at that." Jacob backed his bike up.

"Holy smokes," Clem said, looking down, pulling the cigarette out of his mouth with two fingers. A baby bull snake was gliding out from between the Russian thistle and his boots. It slithered silently across the road.

"I guess it didn't appreciate your jokes."

"You're funny," Clem countered, although he couldn't tell if the kid was joking. "You know anything about that boy who hanged himself?"

47

Jacob squeezed the hand brakes and lifted the bike's front tire up and bounced it on the road a couple of times. He watched the brush swallow the snake on the other side of the road. "He rode on my bus last year. I knew him. A quiet kid."

"I can't understand things like that."

"The whole town is trying to understand." Neither of them looked at each other.

Clem did his tongue lip spit noise, took a long final drag then flicked his cigarette into the road.

"Did you pick that up from old Humphrey Bogart movies?"

"What?"

"Flicking your cigarette away like that."

Clem was surprised. It was such a habit he'd never much thought of it. He let it go. "So how far you riding?"

"Up to the trailhead. I gotta be back at the depot at three." Jacob glanced at his wristwatch. "I'll see ya later." He swung his leg over the bike, lined up the pedal, stood on it, and glided off.

Clem stood there watching the figure bob up the road and out-of-sight. This kid saw right through him. It gave him the creeps and made him feel puny.

Clem knew his persona was a result and a symptom of his past. He kept people at bay or at least arm's length. His caustic way of interacting and not letting people know him or his real mind, probably began in his youth. He was trusting and naïve, like most kids. Behind his back he was known as gullible. He was subjected to pranks and tricks as other kids tested and perfected their power plays. He was teased about his name. He never shared the origins with anyone. He made his mother swear never to divulge the secret. He became leery and callous as he learned the trade of adolescence. The lessons that were passed on from that time were that kids acted the same way when they became adults, just more specialized and devious. It's not that he had become a complete skeptic, but he took everything with a grain of salt now. He thought it funny that as children we are open books, but by adulthood we are locked diaries. We develop distinctive armor along our journey. He couldn't decide whether it really protected him or was a burden to carry all the way to the end. But it had grown on him gradually and imperceptibly. It now fit like an old jacket.

Clem looked up at the sun, then at his wristwatch and remarked, "God damned gone." He turned and walked toward the house. At the same time the dogs quickly rose to follow. He didn't want the kid to see him lollygagging on his way back down the hill.

He reached for the porch post, gripped it and pulled himself up level. His hand came away from the post with paint peelings stuck to it. Remnants of neglect fell to the porch as he swiped his hands together as if playing great cymbals in an orchestra. He made a sweeping circular motion with his head viewing the entire porch from roof to siding to posts to floor planks. He then summed it all up in a disgusted sigh. He looked at the paint chips and with his boot he toed them curiously then mashed them into the planks. He shook his head slowly in a silent resignation to do nothing and entered the house.

The room felt cool against the incessant afternoon heat. Clem was wilting. He flopped into the divan against the wall. As he lay there, he had a bizarre sensation that the spark of life was escaping out through his legs. An electrical tingling moving from his hip, thigh, calf, ankle foot, toes, and . . . gone. Perspiration droplets ran from his temples. He lay there until his heart stopped pounding. The realization of a small panic attack occurred to him.

It was all piling up. He lay there with closed eyes, seeing the pile getting higher and higher. Is this what the mind does when you wander far from order? Drift from routine? Payback for not maintaining civility? Or is it a symptom of the aging process, simply not giving a shit anymore? Maybe it is guilt for not giving a shit, a great big pile of guilt clogging the arteries of reason, reason that has been disintegrating for the past few years. Clem felt sick, as guilt and reason wrestled and somersaulted in his panic. Bad chords were banging away in dissonant cacophonies on the piano of his soul. He tried to hear a melody. He tried to find a tune. It was all sour . . . all dark behind his closed eyes. His heart beat and he started to cry . . . the jaunty little beat of chaos that minds are so good at conjuring. There was a faint desire to go with this fatalistic beat . . . to fall into the easy rhythm of not caring, not believing in tomorrow, letting the beat play out into a fainter and fainter pulse until there was no pulse to believe in, spiraling down into a vortex of white emptiness, devoid of any sound, of any lyrical reason, of anything.

Clem could not find his bootstraps in this whiteout of panic. He was groping for them. He would not succumb to this jaunty little beat. "Pull yourself up. Stop this pathetic pandering to weakness. Get up. Keep going," he heard himself say. It startled him at the thought of a self-engrossed pep talk. Yet he lay there in the beating of his heart, in the soggy panic behind his eyes indulging weakness.

Dogs barking broke the hooks of weakness and Clem came out from behind his eyes. Jacob was riding down the hill on his bike and the dogs asserted themselves in territorial verbal posturing. Clem blinked and sat up.

The dogs were quiet now. The room had sunrays beaming through the south porch windows. Fine dust hovered in the air where Clem sat up. There seemed to be a sizzling of dust stirred up partly because Clem stomped his boots hard on the old Navaho rug and partly from a draft coming from the half-shut front door. He sat on the edge of the divan and steadied himself by gripping the seat cushion. He simply stared into the rays waiting for the moment to pass.

Clem felt funny. The rays were hypnotic. Sunrays always reminded him of sacred moments. The pictures in the Bible. Glorious triumphs noted in history. Walking into a magnificent future or a happy ending. But these were strange. Almost freezing time. The second before a tree falls or a bomb goes off. That stillness in the brief breaths of fear.

He bowed his head looking at the Navaho rug. Rainey had talked him into buying it. *Rainey again.* A sanctuary from the fracas in his head. They bought it from an Indian couple on the plaza in Santa Fe. Rainey loved walking among the Indians and their wares, the silver and turquoise, pottery and rugs, seashell necklaces and sand paintings. She had an affinity for all things Native American. They'd wander the Plaza and she would story-up. Elaborate on ancient trade routes. Explain the significance and origins of the use of coral. The different turquoise mines and their locations. She could describe the matrix found in different turquoises. She knew the symbols in sand paintings and their depictions of gods coming and going. Then, when those stories expired, she moved on to the Hispanic influences of the Santeros and their Retablos, Bultos and Christificatos and touched on the mysterious cult of the Penitentes and their processions of self-flagellation. Sometimes her treasure-trove of trivia became tiresome, but Clem would grin and bear it because he could see that it gave her such pleasure to share what she knew. The glow on her face was irreplaceable. The charm and brilliance of her eyes darting about had a way of creating her unique look and that alone would give Clem relief from all the bits and pieces of information swirling around in his head.

Clem leaned over and picked up the edge of the rug and smelled it. He wanted to return to that time. He slowly shut his eyes and searched the recesses of his memory and waited. The hint of any past was long gone trampled out by the traffic of time and the wear of living. He was finding out that any real proof of her existence in his life was simply in his head. The few knickknacks left were slowly fading and losing any residue of her. The smell of trodden dust was all that remained. He let go of the rug, sat up and looked around the room. Rainey was gone. The storm of passions past had played itself to the last hue of the rainbow now furthest out of reach. Though still, the iridescence and shimmer of her smile remained in a corner of his mind.

Clem was getting weary of this vacillation between comfort and chaos. *I'll rustle up some coffee*, he thought and went to the kitchen. He filled the Paul Revere kettle with water and placed it on the stove. He flipped the burner on and reached for the instant coffee and creamer. From the dish rack he grabbed a mug and placed the items on the kitchen table. Looking around, Clem had to replay where he left the newspaper he bought earlier. Of course, it was still in the truck. As he plodded out the front door Banjo and Sticker nipped his heels with loving wags. The paper was on the floorboard of the cab, disheveled and covered with dusty dog prints. He gathered it, rolled it up and whacked it on his palm with a sound of a firecracker to shoosh the dogs away as he reentered the house. The kettle was boiling when he made it to the kitchen. Silent steam ushered from the spout. The whistle had broken off ages ago. Turning off the stove, Clem lifted the kettle and walked to the table. He filled the mug and returned the kettle to the stove. He sat down and unscrewed the instant coffee, popped the safety seal and spooned it into the mug along with a spoonful of creamer. He stirred the mixture and watched the marbled brown and white swirl make a mini vortex and dissolve. He raised the mug to his lips and slurped. *Hot!* Almost scalding. His eyes teared and he smacked his lips. The heat was a reality check.

Clem scanned the frontpage headlines of the newspaper. A bunch of kids roaming through a pumpkin field took up most of the page. *The pumpkins are pert-near as tall as they were*, he thought. *Was it already time for Halloween? Just god damned gone.* Clem puzzled over the picture and sipped. MAN CLAIMS CIA ABDUCTED HIM, TORTURED THEN DUMPED . . . PRIVATE GUARDS KILL TWO IN IRAQ . . . Clem briefly read bits of the articles and turned the page. Most of the news centered on the war in Iraq. He read that the comedian George Carlin turned 70 and a lawsuit regarding acid rain was settled for 4.6 billion dollars. He turned to the sports page and read that the Rockies had a new star catcher named Yorvit. Clem took another sip. He held the mug close to his lips felt the warm rim. The article triggered a youthful memory about his days in Little League. He held the catcher's position, himself, at twelve. Made the all-star team. He felt that the catcher and pitcher were the best positions in baseball. The most action took place there and they ran the game. Clem looked at his right thumb on the mug. He had broken it twice misjudging balls. He knew it was better to keep it behind his back but always got anxious when a stolen base was at stake. He peeked over and wiggled his thumb. The skin was tight around it. The skin was tight and swollen around all his fingers and joints. He could hardly get his finger in the handle of the mug they were so bulbous. *All those years of working with your hands will do it,* he figured. *Life wears you out before you know it.* He sipped the last of the dark liquid from the mug and flipped to the obituary section. Maybe there was something about the kid who hung himself. A funeral or memorial service. But no, nothing.

Clem folded the paper and laid it on the table. He rose, went to the stove, picked up the kettle, returned to the table and filled his mug with water. He repeated the teaspoon of instant coffee and creamer, stirred it once and watched the marbled-brown and white swirl do its mini vortex and dissolve. He put the kettle on the stove and sat back down. The coffee was not so hot this time. He sipped and stared into space.

He had never thought about dying when he was young. For every bad situation that occurred he would come up with a solution. In fact the problem of the solution was the challenge he looked forward to conquering. The "fix it" syndrome he reckoned. As a youngster, whenever Clem was feeling down his father would say, "now, now, it's not that bad, things have a way of working themselves out." In his father's fix-all advice there lay a standard instant conversational addendum so commonplace it is lost by those it is intended for. "…a way of working themselves out." It is this last inference that is the most poignant lesson Clem had taken solace in. But he remembered there was an additional adage he'd heard his father sometimes say, "…with or without your help." This phrase was what Clem gravitated to. It would be *with* his help. He would influence the outcome somehow. He would help along his destiny and not let blind fate run amok.

So long ago in the immortality of youth and the garden of trust a child has for their parents, there lies a golden path to the future. A child's blank slate that bears the fruits of endless possibilities is fragile and needs to be tended with love and handled with care. "The dots were out of whack," Clem whispered, "the kid just didn't connect the dots." In Clem's mind *the dots* were the essential building blocks for a solid foundation in the house of life. When a dot was missing, he searched for, or substituted another dot and kept going. Clem knew he was speculating on the kid's reasons. What did he know of this child's life, or family, or upbringing? Zilch! Was he focusing on this unknown dilemma because of his own crux? Clem knuckled his nose and snorted in disgust. *Gadzooks, I gotta find the next dot*, he repeated in his mind.

Clem stuck his bulbous digit in the mug handle and lifted it to his lips and sipped. He almost gagged. The coffee was cold now. Had he been *that* consumed with the past and his war with time? "The mind is a magician that halts or accelerates time," is what Rainey used to say. He was always befuddled by the way time seemed to quicken the older you got. He recalled summer days under apricot trees in his parents' backyard. The days were eternal. He would collect the soft round wonders that had fallen for his mother's pies. He would bite into the best ones relishing in the sweet sticky juices. The hot summer air watched him dodge the bees and black ants that shared split ones on the hot summer bricks. Even the black flies were slower back then. He hated the way it all seemed to be condensed into a black and white snapshot and filed away into a scrapbook with a bow of Time tied around it. This battle of past, present, and future and how it intermingled like a Twilight Zone horror was becoming a living nightmare. *I gotta find the next dot,* he repeated silently.

There've been times when the kitchen had sounds or colors or a feeling that Clem would suddenly sense, and he would look up. More so just after Rainey left. Her presence had lingered, or rather, his want of her presence persisted. He'd begin a conversation in his head daring himself to start aloud. Then peer up at the ghostly starkness of the chair, bleak and still. His gut would churn with involuntary memories. He now sat there in that spectral haze with a lost, dopey expression. He'd left her placemat and a mug there almost as an invitation for her with everyday a wishful expectation. The placemat had faded from the sunlight of many mornings. He'd rinsed the mug occasionally.

Clem pushed his chair back from the table in a linoleum-verses-metal screech. He rinsed his mug and put away the coffee and creamer. He decided the next dot would be ordering a new waterheater. In a drawer next to the icebox he found a notepad and pencil. He walked to the laundry room where the water heater was located. A quick inspection gave him the size, wattage and gallons. He hoped he could replace it with the same, so as not to have re-plumbing issue but anticipated the worst. No standardization anymore, a curse of capitalism. The slogan, "New and Improved" streamed by. He noted that the water heater had been purchased from the local True Value hardware store in Colorado City. After jotting down the information Clem went to the desk in the hallway. He opened the drawer and lifted the telephone book out and found the number. He dialed and got an automated message regarding store hours and days. He stood there with his mouth gaping. "God and the universe are in cahoots against me," he said, slamming down the receiver and tossing the phonebook back in the drawer. Absentmindedly he shuffled through the discarded mail by the phone. Big mistake. There were several overdue notices regarding his truck and three letters from his landlord. He looked at his wristwatch and it indicated 5:30 PM.

The room had the western sunlight filtering in and there was a faint sound of a scratch at the back screen door. The dogs. Clem spun around and clomped to the backdoor, pushed it open. Banjo and Sticker scrambled past doing a Laurel-and-Hardy squeeze between Clem's leg and the door jamb. As he stood there, he felt the sunrays hit his face. He gazed at the way the light saturated the field, illuminating it in contrast to the dark-shaded Wet Mountains to the north. *If time stood still, it stood still here*, Clem thought, *when I die, I want to come back as this field. Men live and die too quickly*. To be the convergence of man's wonder had a rather satisfying appeal to it. An inner smile tingled around his heart. Another dot had arrived.

He took a quick peek at the field as the yellow orb ducked below the mountain ridge and let the screen door ease back into place. Clem marched upstairs to his bedroom and gathered all the clothes on the floor and chairs then to the bathroom for towels and miscellaneous undergarments strewn about. With his arms full he made his way back downstairs to the laundry room. Dropping the bundle in front of the washing machine he waited a moment huffing. He lifted the lid of the washer and set the dial on Heavy Load. Then he opened the cabinet above, reached for the detergent, dumped what he reckoned was a cup's worth, called it good and put the box back on its shelf. Next he separated colors and whites. Then he gathered the colored clothes up and stuffed them into the wash drum. He even stripped down adding his shirt, trousers and socks to the mix. Cold water or not, he would have clean clothes.

After closing the lid, he placed both hands on the edges of the washer. He listened to it fill and waited for the wash cycle to begin. When the machine kicked into wash he turned and walked into the kitchen wearing only his straw hat and white jockey shorts. The dogs were sitting in front of the sink staring up at him. "What in the hell are you looking at?" he smirked. Their rumps wiggled. Clem shooshed them out the back screendoor embarrassed in his skimpy attire and came back to the kitchen.

The linoleum felt cool under his feet. He wiggled his toes and instinctively felt for his cigarettes. All he got were chest hairs. "Shit! God-damn, son of a bitch." Clem scrambled for the laundry room, hit the dial while flinging the lid open. The cigarette pack was floating in a bubbly foam. He reached in and rescued it, desperately hoping they weren't completely soaked. He tore open the pack and to his relief only the first four were saturated. Apparently, the pack had immediately floated to the surface giving the cigarettes a chance to survive. He then rushed to the kitchen countertop and dissected the pack. He extracted each individual cigarette and inspected it for moisture. He placed them in a row based on saturation levels. Having accomplished that, he took the last one and stuck it in his lips, found a lighter on the kitchen table, put flame to it and took a drag. Clem wanted to blame the dots for sidetracking him, but he knew he couldn't. He had to tough it out and mentally kicked himself for colossal stupidity. He smoked and put the mishap aside, rationalizing the whole event by his saving the rest of the pack.

Clem knocked an ash into the sink and went upstairs for his bathrobe. He pulled the robe belt and snugged it, then entered his bedroom tossing his hat on the chair. He fell onto the bed and sat there bouncing twice. He smoked and half-grinned while a cloud of dots circled him. The room was stifling. The day's heat had concentrated in the upstairs room. The bedcovers had a *just-ironed* warmth to them. The air penetrated his entire being. He smoked on and gave another bounce. The window was shut. The room needed to breathe. He needed to breathe but he was stuck. He wished he could open it with telekinesis. Finally, he slipped off the bed and unlatched the window and heaved it up. Immediately smoke and hot air were sucked out. He felt tired again. More than that, he felt exhausted. He looked out the window at the fading light then snubbed his butt out in an ashtray on the bedside table. Walking back around the bed he sat on the edge and bounced gently. He felt light wafts of air brush across his face on their way out the window. He leaned back onto his pillow and stared at the ceiling. Spider webs trembled in the draft. He followed cracks in the wall with his eyes. He listened to his heartbeat. A black fly buzzed in circles above him. Its repetitive motion lulled him into RaineyLand...

*In a 50's style diner booth they sat opposite each other looking at a fly hovering above their breakfast burrito plates. The White Spot Café in downtown Trinidad had been recommended as the best place to eat for the price. They had come down the night before, got a room and spent the evening in the bar at the Best Western having a few too many margaritas. The next morning, both were green-bellied and wobbly-legged. It was still early, and they were to meet a horse breeder at noon and had time to kill. "You think he'll land?" Rainey asked. "Put some of that Dave's Insanity hot sauce on your burrito and he won't." Clem suggested. She picked the bottle up and read the back label out loud, "Will strip wax off floors. Removes grease stains on driveways. Hottest sauce in the universe." She untwisted the cap and doused her burrito. He appreciated the fact that she was not squeamish. They both ate and looked around commenting on coat hanger polls on either end of the booth and the black and white squares on the floor. Clem liked the blue vinyl seats and said they reminded him of a '65 Thunderbird he owned once, comfortable small talk.*

*The waitress moved like a shark swimming in and out of booths and the aisle, snapping up plates and tips. She floated up to their booth with a thermos filled with coffee saying, "You look like you could use this," and left it on the table. The radio in the kitchen was tinkling Ozzie Ozborn and our waitress told us the cook was her husband. He had a black ponytail and tattoos ran the length of his arms like a long sleeve shirt. You could see his black leather vest under his apron filled with badges from poker runs and various swastikas. Rainey liked the place, said it had a hard charm about it. "Uncomplicated color" was how she put it. It was the way she could see the uniqueness of everything that he admired. They were hung over but excited about life then... The* fly circled and circled. He closed his eyes and slept.

Several hours passed and Clem opened his eyes. It was dark in the room. He remembered that he'd fallen asleep. He rolled over on his side and leaned out of bed. He had to pee. His mouth tasted sour and was dry. He groaned and stood up. The dogs were not on the rug next to the bed, so he didn't have to step over them on the way to the toilet. To and from the bathroom he didn't bother to turn on a light. He had the house memorized. He took off his robe and this time crawled under the covers. The room had cooled off. He tried not to lasso any one thought for fear of worrying about it. He lay there in human silence and tried to breath.

Then began the tossing and turning, searching for an optimal position of comfort.

Arm bent under the pillow.

No.

Adjust the pillow higher.

No.

Arm outstretched.

No.

More pillow.

No.

Turn over.

No.

Other side, curl feet up…

He began to envision a Pez dispenser, the early candy contraption made of bright colored plastic that ejected small cubes of colored sweets. It was his first fascination with mechanical devices. In fact, Clem still had one from his youth. It was in a cigar box along with his father's wristwatch and some baby teeth. He wasn't exactly sentimental, nor did he believe in karma, but he had hung onto it for the mere sake of it. Maybe it was that it helped him remember his beginnings, where he'd come from, a grounding to keep him honest. He counted the colored Pez bricks like sheep going over a wooden rail fence. He ejected them, making them shoot across his dreamscape room and fly out the window. He made them different colors. He even ate one or two. He made it so he didn't have to reload, just endless Pez candies soaring through his dreamscape. He reached sixty-seven and was beginning to lose track. He thought one of them tasted like perfume. He saw Rainey catch one and throw it at him. They played catch together in a psychedelic Pez-filled dreamscape. He tried to get closer to her, but she lobbed one over his head and he turned to fetch it. When he turned around, she was gone. He was holding the Pez in his hand and it dissolved, he was gripping the vanishing Pez dust with his bulbous fingers and fading into sleep.

# Three
## Thursday, 12th Morning

*She was calling his name in a soft white silence. He waited and then heard it twice more. He was trying to find her and the way down. He stumbled and cursed and stumbled again and the voice repeated in the strange white. This white of engrossing pleasure kept him searching and waiting. It was Rainey and she was calling to him. Now all the white was changing to a colorful pink, now red, now brown, now dark and it wasn't her voice any longer. It was another sound familiar and repeating twice more and he waited. He thought he was on the mesa. Wasn't she there? Yes. Clem was moving his hand and trying to reach her but it wouldn't move. He was . . .* waking up. No! No!

He heard the sound again. His eyes were opening, and he lay there depressed at only a dream.

He had an erection that was melting. A crow was cawing in the field outside his window. He knew it now. He swallowed dry, closed his eyes hard and hurried to relive some bit of the dream, turning over and burying his head in the pillow watching the two of them standing on the edge of the mesa looking out over the valley.

It was years ago, back when they had just recently met, that he had talked her into hiking to the top of Starvation Peak in New Mexico. It was something they could do together *and* be outdoors. The climb took thirty minutes on that clear magical day. They talked and made their way through piñon, cedar, prickly pear and yucca. When they made the summit, both had the impulse to make love on the smooth flat volcanic rocks. The sun burned their skin and little ants bit them and they sweated, and sand stuck to their flesh. Spontaneous ecstasy was never more perfect than this. They fell apart and lay there, enjoying. They talked about the incident that gave this mesa its name. A 17th century legion of Spaniards that was attacked by marauding Indians and forced to flee to the mesa's crest where they were then starved out. Rainey was keen on local stories and Clem loved to listen to her talk and watch her. She had found an arrowhead on the climb and gave it to him. He envied her luck in finding it. He had looked his whole life and never come close. It was one of the few things he had kept for all these years, a worthless piece of stone shrouded in a beautiful memory.

Dawn crept up in grays. The crows had gone, and Clem lay there. He scratched his chin and felt the stubble. The dream was like too much coffee. Things were going haywire in his head. Answers, too late, came by the truckload and there was nowhere to dump 'em. He lay there in the quagmire of things to do and fidgeted. Bile and a metallic taste crept from his esophagus.

He flung the covers aside and bent out of bed. His ankles clicked as he walked to the bathroom. He looked at himself in the mirror and tentatively touched the wattle of skin under his chin. He would dry-bathe and shave and start his day, again.

Downstairs the dogs were scratching at the back door. Clem had risen late, much later than usual. He opened the door and they raced past him to their bowls, stubs wagging. Clem got a whiff of skunk. He went for the bag of kibble and poured some in the bowls giving each dog a short sniff. He surmised that the little devils had dodged any significant spray and were safe to be in the house. He returned the bag and walked to the laundry room. He threw another load of clothes in the washer, this time half the whites, adjusted the setting and started it.

At the stove he turned a flame on under the kettle of water and pulled down the instant coffee and creamer from the cupboard. He rinsed a dirty mug from the sink using his fingers then shook it. He stood there with *have a good day* looping in his head. He repeated his coffee and creamer routine stirring robotically listening to the calming ping of the spoon against the mug, raised it to his lips and slurped. He smacked his tongue against the roof of his mouth and gasped a comfort sigh. The chugging rhythm of the washer helped his mind whittle at the to-do-list this morning.

A fried egg on toast was in the works as he had his second cup of coffee and cigarette. He wasn't much hungry but decided he had better eat so as not to have to listen to his stomach growl.

Clem finished eating and piled plate, pan, cup and utensils in the sink. He then emptied the washer of clothes into a wicker basket that held the colored clothes of the previous day. Hefting it, he made his way out the back door to the clothesline with the dogs at his heels. Clothespins were hanging in a cloth bag on the line. They were sun-bleached and warped with age but worked. He shook each garment out and hung them in a chain, economizing clothespins as he went. As he worked, the dream and Rainey came and went.

After the clothes were hung, Clem moseyed over to the corral. He leaned against the rails watching magpies zigzag in the warm currents above the yellow field. The pure luminous field always made him feel the presence of God or a heavenly magnificence. Most of the old timers referred to this area as God's country. "Shit, wasn't it *all* God's country," he quibbled. The past few days he had been picking at his beliefs. He'd been turning them over and thinking about the other side. The heavy-tailed magpies flapped their wings some, then sank in the air and flapped again and sank until they flew behind tall pines. He saw the dogs chasing each other.

*Maybe belief systems are as old as mankind itself.* He figured prehistoric man looked at the skies and wondered. Their first questions of the unknown made good campfire chat. *Why am I?* and *Death* probably got lots of attention. After walking upright and making tools and fire, the ball really started rolling. Then the stories began. Stories of the sun, moon, and stars. Stories handed down from one generation to the next. Clem laughed at the idea of oral tradition and how his friends constantly told tall tales and each one taller the next time it was told. Maybe the telling of stories became a tradition in itself and the storyteller became sacred in some way. *How it all panned out was anyone's guess*, Clem pondered. Maybe the telling of stories and having to remember them had something to do with man's mind and development of his brain. Intelligence was man's foothold like the eagle's eyes. *The skills to communicate really must have snowballed back then*, Clem spit. All those stories and accumulated knowledge became darned important and those that retained that stuff were revered and powerful. In school he learned that Egyptians and Greeks had lots of gods representing things like the sun, thunder, ocean, mountains and lots more he couldn't think of. They also had lots of slaves. He recalled by the medieval times the church and priest held all books of knowledge and were often the only ones who could read, the up side to that was they held all the power. Clem knew his upbringing and influences were based on an organized religious system of beliefs. But what did *he* believe? No one had ever asked him. He had taken it for granted that he believed, but it was the constant indoctrination and the hyper-familiarity that caused him to believe. The practice of "compare and contrast" in Catholicism was not an option for an adolescent. There was no reason to doubt. But he soon had doubt and questions arose. He just left the church and organized religion one day and hadn't given it much thought since. Clem had a hard time talking with others about religion and God. It became endless babble and he felt it never went anywhere. Everybody's religion had answers, but they never really jived with his. Every conversation ended incomplete and unfulfilling, so he avoided them. He knew for certain that all the answers he heard sparked new questions and other ways of looking at things.

There were two fifty-cent words he had learned in Sunday sermons that always impressed him, omnipotent and omniscient. It bugged him no end that if god were endowed with these powers what was the point of choice? Was it all a great dream of the unanswerable? A revolving door going nowhere? Always looking for something that was never where you left it? Was it simpler to just believe and get it over with? Clem knew he wasn't wired that way. He was a hands-on man. He believed in earth's natural laws. He believed in what his senses told him. He believed in all that he had experienced throughout his life. He did not believe in all he read because the victor wrote the history and what had the vanquished to say? What you do is what you believe. Points of view had thirty-one flavors and he was a coconut man and

Baskin-Robbins had discontinued that flavor because of ever-changing public taste. He knew he wasn't alone or else there wouldn't be so many religions popping up. He also knew the more you know the more you find you don't know. Who can retain all knowledge? He giggled underneath his breath and said "*computers*" as a mental comic relief. Then the phrase "moths to a flame" popped into his mind. Could it be the screens of computers, televisions, and Game Boys are the modern-day flame replacing man's ancient attraction to fire and the stories told around it?

There wasn't a day that went by that Clem didn't close his eyes and offer up a silent prayer of thanks to a universal spirit for each day of his life, and with each prayer, he felt at ease and a sense of relinquishment. In those moments all earthbound worries vanished. He had found some little peace that worked for him. There was something driving him to find his own way. Finding his own truth and virtues had come in shifts and jerks, through hard knocks and heartache, through day-in and day-out and getting up every morning and looking out the window. The idea of certain traditions being obsolete crossed his mind. Living by popular clichés also crossed his mind. He guessed the few things he had taken with him from his travails in Catholicism were that Jesus preached love and that the kingdom of heaven was within you. Maybe it was that simple.

He could hear a truck coming from an upper ranch, gliding almost silently down the hill, a smooth sound like a long wave. He heard a bell, probably a rock hitting the fender well of the trailer. It almost sounded like the United Methodist Church bell with its call to commune. Tradition, religion and spirituality kept hammering away at Clem's thoughts, Western Theology dominant. The Mormon, Catholic, Methodist, Baptist, Church of Christ and other denominations all busy preaching, communing, guiding and informing every Sunday, yet hypocrisies scurried around all the rest of the week.

Clem scraped dirt off his boot against the bottom rail and spat. Looking out that window at the carpet of yellow gave him a centering. Looking out at the field now helped with his search. This was truth. All that had been and all to come was in these fields. The wind and the rain spoke louder than words. "We better enjoy what time we have here for what it is and stop bitchin' an' moanin'," he spit again, still scraping his boot, watching smithereens of dirt fall.

Clem had a sudden flash. An image of his high school science teacher and something he'd said came to mind. All the chemicals in the galaxy are created from stars like the sun. It all had to do with the heating up and splitting of atoms. They all floated out into space. Clem thought of the stardust that fairies sprinkle on you.

The morning sun sprinkled warmth onto Clem's back. Clem did not have all the answers. That was today's certain truth. He craved a cigarette but had left the row of laundered cigarettes like bullets on the kitchen counter waiting to fire. He smelled the air and its dryness. The hot weather will subside with the coming of winter's snow he knew. Long anticipated and wished for, the moisture is needed because the entire valley is a tinderbox ready to burst into flame. The deer are sporting new velvet antlers and leaves have that yellow tinge of coming autumn. At night he could smell the pungent odor of hungry bears scavenging for anything to fatten up for hibernation. He looked at his apple trees that have been a regular stop for feasting. *They've broken so many branches that I'll have to prune 'em or loose 'em,* he thought. But they would have to wait.

Clem thought about the meaning of life. He felt the meaning was everywhere you looked. One only had to acknowledge it and not wait for something to conk you on the head. He had seen eagles talon prairie dogs, turkeys scurry across the road, and great blue herons wing from valley ponds. He had heard bull elk bellow and coyotes yip in the hills. It was a matter of living he figured. His greatest sin was not living enough. He knew it. He hadn't pushed himself. Things were all too easy and his humanity was soft. This guilt he had.

As he stared down at the dust filtering into the stalks of golden grass, Clem remembered a story he had heard when he first moved here, told by Mr. Willie Bust. Mr. Bust . . . everyone referred to him as "The Saddle Man" because he collected saddles and anything Indian or Western-related, a crusty and colorful man. Blond hair, glacial blue eyes and a weathered face dried by hot time. He had a small cowboy museum attached to the back of his house and he loved to tell stories. He once had an amazing collection of eagle-feathered Indian head bonnets until the government forced him to give them up. Clem couldn't remember if the story was legend or lore, but it was a good story. Willie spoke in an unassuming folksy manner with enough drawl so that, as the stories unfolded, you could picture him actually there. This particular story of Willie's had taken place a hundred or so years before. The skeletal remains of a Comanche hunter were found sprawled next to a slain Grizzly bear full of arrows. The brave had claw marks across his skull and breastbone. Both must have bled to death during a struggle in the field near Clem's ranch. Willie's story resonated with Clem. From then on he likened his field to the Elysian Fields, a happy otherworld for heroes favored by the gods according to the Greeks. A kind of heaven-like place you went to after being killed in battle. The yellow field was this Comanche's resting place. Clem wondered if the Comanche's eyes were open or closed when he died. Did he feel honor in battling this impressive animal? Did he see the grizzly take its last breath?

Clem spit in frustration. His boot slipped from the corral rail. The metal rails were hot to the touch and you could see the distortion of air as the heat rose and wiggled. The sun was heating everything, and time was becoming a mirage of life's purpose. Clem instantly shivered for a second, spit twice, turned and shuffled to the shed.

Pushing open the dilapidated shed door, Clem saw only bright dazzling phantoms as his eyes adjusted to the darkness. Flipping the light switch, he surveyed the space. His mission was to locate the chainsaw for Jean's brother and inspect it. He desperately needed to get busy.

The shed was packed to the gills with assorted tools, hardware, mowers, and junk. Mostly junk. He had been a collector. He could see plainly that the days of collecting were over. It would take the rest of his life just to get rid of it all. What he could really use right now was a water heater and that was not what was among the collectibles. He'd saved certain items with the clear understanding that you have to wait long enough to need them. Was he waiting for retirement from a career of rat packing? What needed collecting now was time.

As he made his way to the rear of the shed where the chainsaw was hanging, he kicked rusted gas cans and enmeshed himself in fallen balls of twine. He stamped and shook his feet and the twine fell away.

Bat guano and dust covered everything. He lifted the saw from the hook, laid it on the nearby bench and found a rag. Clem swept the rag back and forth over the saw. Bat droppings and dust scattered every which-a-way making the rays of light from the open door come alive.

"It's not bad," he said. He inspected and unscrewed the fuel cap. The tank was empty which meant he'd drained it before storage so the carburetor would not resin up. He found a can of premixed gas underneath the bench, then filled the fuel tank and screwed the cap back on. Next he checked the bar and chain oil reservoir, dipping his little finger in. It was low. He found the chain oil where the gas can had been and topped it off. Clem ran his fingers over the chain lightly feeling the edges for sharpness. "Not bad," he spit into the dust ridden rays, "but I'll check the plug," he murmured. Socket wrench and fittings were there in a cubby next to the bench. Pulling the boot and wire off, he unscrewed the plug and peered at the gap. It was clean of carbon. Next he located a compression gauge and inserted it into the sparkplug chamber and pulled the chord. It indicated that the ring and piston still held a decent seal. For good measure he pulled the air filter and cleaned it of saw dust and inspected it for holes. He then reassembled the parts and with great strides made his way out of the shed.

Out in the warm brightness he blinked and found a stump to rest the saw on. Clem stood there with his hands on his back haunches and stretched, groaning. He swiped his forehead and looked at the sweat on the back of his hand. In the microscope of day, he saw the sweat highlight the ravages that time had inflicted on his spotted skin. He wiped his hand on his trousers and twitched. He craved a cigarette and patted his pockets.

Clem bent over the saw and pulled the chord. The saw engine popped, turned over and spouted a bit of smoke but failed to start. "Old gas," was his conclusion. He went back to the shed to find a can of starting fluid. Unscrewing the air filter and pulling out the choke, he shot a couple of quick squirts into the carburetor. He pulled the rope. The engine screamed to the tune of a thousand tap dancing firecrackers. He squeezed the throttle and it screamed louder.

Clem grinned.

He laid the saw on the stump and watched it shake and rattle. For a moment the saw emitted a very light hazy blue smoke then it cleared. The steady popping was a pleasing sound. Clem nodded and flipped the kill switch. With deftness he replaced the air filter cover and carried the saw back into the shed. "Jean's brother would be satisfied with this saw," he agreed with himself.

He left the shed and closed the door behind him. He walked to the back door of the house through the crunch and swishing sounds of the tall dry grass. He swung the screen door open and went into the kitchen. He went directly for the counter and the row of "bullets." He selected one, lit it and puffed. Nicotine ran through his bloodstream.

He settled down and wiped the sweat from his forehead. He was trying to connect the dots this morning. Somehow, he felt he was only retracing a trail of old dots. What exactly was his path? He was unsure. Was he headed the right way? He feared some paths could not be altered. Some directions could not be changed. Certain courses are inevitable because the captain follows his chart. Sextons and positions, calculations and decisions all play roles in the final destination towards the horizon with a hopeful pinpointed accuracy that is anything but accurate, the fatal flaw of self-destruction. How does the shepherd tend his mighty flock of uncontrollable self-doubt and insecurities? Clem was being bullied by his own thoughts. He followed the dots with confidence then cowered at their seemingly meaningless connection to his life . . . a

79

habitual follower of past behavior that he despises and no longer understands as relevant. He is treading on new ground that age has now bequeathed to him. The young man he'd once been was now obsolete. A new creature from the seed of perspective was evolving. The young man could only be used as a reference and possible footnote.

Clem shook his head violently and the cigarette dropped an inch-long ash to the countertop. This thing that had gripped him, this potion he accidentally drank could not be undone. He took a deep drag off the cigarette and steadied himself. "God damn. Slow down. You're trying too hard." The words flowed out in a smoky murmur. "Stay on track. You keep going."

He decided to stop listening to his inner voice. He craved a comfort zone. If it was old habits then so be it. He put the cigarette in his mouth and walked to the phone in the hallway. He looked up Jean Stanley's number, picked up the receiver and dialed. It rang ten times and he was about to hang up when a groggy voice finally answered.

"Hey, Miss Muffin, I hope I didn't wake you."

"Who is this?"

"It's the Lottery Jury. It has come to our attention that you are the winner of 300 million in the Power Ball."

"God Damn it, Clem, what the hell do you want."

"Come on now don't be that way."

"This better be good."

"Just wanted to give you the heads-up on the Stihl."

"Yeah?"

"She's tuned, cleaned, and runs like a champ. Pulled her out this morning and fired her up and she's smooth as can be, so pass it on to your brother and have him call me. You still got my number, huh?"

"Yeah, but if you don't let me get back to my beauty sleep, I'm gonna throw it away."

"All right, sweetie, but you don't need no beauty sleep. You're beautiful wide awake."

The phone went dead and then a dial tone started. Clem held the receiver and grinned. He looked at the butt between his fingers and then pinched it. Clem needed the money.

"I'll kill two birds with one stone," he'd check again with True Value about a water heater. He dialed. Automated message. He looked at his wristwatch. 7:30. "Come on, where are you people?" He moaned while the overdue notices glared up at him from the tabletop.

Clem waited there pinching the butt. Out of left field he thought of Jeans' voice. "Her voice don't match her looks. That's a darn shame," he commented to himself. Then out of the blue he thought Rainey's voice was a perfect match to her looks, a rusty satin quality that even now brought a rustle to Clem's groin. Maybe that's why he loved to hear her stories. He was shifting in and out of emotional wormholes, traveling vast expanses to past experiences triggered by the vivid reality of his current situation. He laid the receiver down and moved toward the backdoor. Nausea gripped him unexpectedly. He wasn't going to vomit, but it was dire he get some fresh air immediately. With labored steps he reached the screen door and grasped it, holding on. Slowly he squatted down on the concrete walkway outside. He was lightheaded. There was a spin and tiny glints of light-spots floating in his eyes. Then it passed as quick as it had come. From where he sat it was enough just to gaze at the yellow field. The morning sun cast a gold richness onto the grasses. Clem felt blessed. If this was his last view before the sweet bye-and-bye, that would be fine by him.

Clem rose and made his way weakly to the kitchen sink. He pulled a glass from the cupboard and filled it with water and drank. The water was cool. His eyes closed. He swallowed in slow gulps breathing between. He put the glass down on the counter without opening his eyes. He lingered and licked his lips. *Rainey had kissed with her eyes open*, he remembered. He had asked her one time, why? She explained that it was to witness the closeness and to verify intimacy, to feel it and to see it, to be there at the exact moment in love. He had thought it typically peculiar of her and let it go. She could get all the verification she wanted; he would keep his eyes shut. He licked his lips again still with eyes shut. If he opened them the swirling, tumbling cascade of junk would start dumping on him, so he waited, waiting there in the brief flash of Rainey color behind his eyes.

After a minute or so his eyes opened. The room was not moving. He decided he felt reasonably well. "Let's get a move on here," he whispered. He had a plan. The plan would entail cutting the last bit of fall hay in the field. Clem launched himself towards the back screendoor.

# Four
## Thursday, 12th  1:15 PM

As the tractor rattled along, a light breeze blew east from off the mountain. Heat and breeze alternated in the brilliance of the afternoon. The bounce and rock the tractor produced was a lulling and hypnotic motion. The clothes on the line lifted then fell in gentle waves like someone saying goodbye. Clem turned his head looking at this picture. His entire small world was in sync, a collective breathing of the planet and his existence; the dry yellow stems swaying, the Appaloosa's flicking tail, islands of clouds passing above. All could be seen at once in macro consciousness. The turning of drive shaft and ping of pistons were clearly audible. The individual scythe-strokes struck a wonderful rhythm. Clem was smirking in this symphony of familiar sounds. The pleasant zone seemed to grow wider and included trees, boulders, the curling tarpaper on the out-sheds. Clem's senses were telescopic. He could pick out milkweed bugs lighting on the barn boards, mud swallows jetting up in the dry currents. He scented the vanilla of ponderosa pines. The yellow field's musk of sage, grama grass, and dried clover assaulted him. He inhaled as if he were buried in Rainey's lovely hair.

Then another sound started foreign to this temporary bliss. The wrong kind of sound that goes to the pit of the stomach. A sound with attachments to fear and dread. A sound that can only mean one thing and one thing only. A sound that you want desperately to ignore but experience forces you to listen and replay the sound over and over instantly in your head. Then there was a jolt, and in that moment, Clem was thrust forward then regained his seating. The tractor wobbled and the swather jerked and hesitated. Clem's blissful symphony now was a wounded metal grinding dissonance. Metallic screams washed in agony, echoed. The harmony he'd been enjoying a few moments ago had just died. Then the cryptic noise was gone. The machinery trudged on. "What the hell was that?" he cried. In his disbelief he turned his head to look back. All that was evident was a quickly fading puff of dust. *Just the head of that old orphan boulder*, he thought. Clem looked at his hands on the steering wheel and squeezed hard on the grip. He could swear he had had a cigarette between his knuckles but was in perplexed doubt. An overriding impulse to stop and investigate began in him. He did not want to deal with it. Did not want to be faced with anything more. He'd forgotten about where that boulder was. He subconsciously searched for a hill of sand, for a hole to bury his head in.

Clem was rounding the western most part of the field enclosed by a barbed wire fence line. He yanked on the steering wheel turning it to the left. Something caught his eye. A strange, alien color flashed. He blinked, but it flashed again, then again. He squinted and stopped the tractor, staring at the swath he had just cut. Colossal disbelief froze him.

*Fire.*

The loop accelerated in his mind.

Clem was running. His stare was fixed on the phantom of dancing orange. He ran faster, stumbling, regaining balance. Panting and running. Tasting his dehydrated tongue. Praying for a prayer to come to him. Running towards the terrible orange that now was red.

*1:45 PM*

As Clem neared the red, translucent rivulets of white smoke were ascending to the heavens. He hadn't a clue what to do. Clem took his hat off and began beating the area that was ablaze.

At first, he felt he was getting the upper hand. He beat and stomped in a furious manner. He flung handfuls of dirt and patted the burning grass maniacally with his palms. His lungs were singed and filling with smoke. He fitfully coughed. He stepped back away from the smoke and heat to catch fresh air. The smoke was thick from the smoldering grass and it chased him. An errant wind gusted past and moved the smoke towards the eastern rise. Clem shuttered. The fire was spreading and was sprinting towards a patch of pine trees nearby. There were no prayers to be had now.

He turned. Stunned. Then slowly jogged, struggling towards the house. "Call someone," he murmured and picked up the pace. He spun around in a continuous motion to glimpse at the fire. "Oh my god!" as he ran faster. By the time he reached the backdoor he was staggering and gasping. He opened the door and the dogs shimmied by and he ricocheted off the hall wall and slid to a halt at the phone.

2:15 PM

Receiver in hand he dialed 911. The voice of a woman answered.

"Pueblo County 911 what is your emergency?"

"I got a fire," he bellowed into the receiver.

"What address?

"Up on Cuerno Verde road in Rye."

"May I have your name?"

"Clem Everett. It's a grass fire on my property here in Rye."

"Mr. Everett this fire has been reported and we have units that have been dispatched. The Local fire district has been notified and are currently responding."

"Yeah, but it's headed up the hill."

"Are there dwellings in the immediate vicinity?"

"There are a couple of houses just over the ridge."

"Can you stay on the line? I will check the status of the fire units."

"Yeah sure."

Clem waited and coughed.

"Mr Everett?"

"Yeah."

"Fire units should arrive shortly."

"O.K. I'll go out front."

He pitched the receiver and dashed through the front door. The dogs met him and scrambled along behind. On the front porch he could hear the sirens coming up the dirt road. Several cars had stopped, and their occupants were getting out to look at the blaze as if it were a Disney attraction, busily clicking off pictures on their cell phones. Clem ran into the field and realized with mounting horror he'd left the tractor running. He turned the key and the engine quit. He looked at the fire. It had traveled up to tree line and some scrub oaks were already ablaze. The gray-white smoke billowed into the sky. Clem looked at the fire then turned to the house and then to the shed and barn. The horse was kicking its heels in the air and whinnying. Clem hurried to the gate and opened it then dashed to the shed for the lead rope and bridle. He then moved cautiously to the Appaloosa trying to be as calm as possible. Her eyes were as wide as his. He slowly put the bridle on and led the horse to the upper pasture on the northwest side of his house. He opened the gate and led the horse in and unhooked the bridle, swatted the horse's rump and gave a yell, "git." It galloped off; its tail whirling behind it.

The first to arrive was a structural truck mainly equipped to deal with house fires. The unit chief hopped out to assess the situation. Some personnel at the station working on vehicles had seen the smoke on Rattlesnake Hill and thought it was a controlled burn, so when they arrived, they were not prepared for a grass fire soon to become a forest fire. The truck only held 1,500 to 2,000 gallons of water, not nearly enough for a fire of this magnitude. The chief immediately determined backup was needed. Clem was running towards the truck as the chief radioed to the station house. As Clem approached, the chief yelled something about an entry point and Clem waved him in the direction of a sagging barbed wire gate. He went to the gate and unhooked it, threw it open and frantically waved for the truck to enter. The truck had overshot the gate and had to back up. The chief was still on his handheld radio communicating to the station. He conveyed that the situation was worsening by the second due to winds feeding the fire. The Pueblo West Station and the Forest Service had already been alerted and were responding but would take at least forty-five minutes to arrive. The structural truck roared past Clem and parked. The chief jumped out and sprinted over to him wanting to know if there were any other entrances on the other side of the ridge in the case that they needed to relocate equipment to create a fire break. Clem went blank for a moment and then replied, "Spencer's."

"Spencer's," The Chief repeated.

"Yeah, off 165 just past Old San Isabel Road on the left."

"Is there an address?"

"I don't know it . . . but there's a big old iron gatepost with the name "Spencer's" on top."

The Chief was back on the radio giving orders and walking towards the truck. He shouted out directions and men began removing hoses, pickaxes and shovels from the side and back of the truck. They had parked the vehicle at an area charred black, the origin of the fire, at the base of a small hill that rose into a grove of Ponderosa pines. Clem stood back aghast at the scene unfolding before him. He had to put his hand on a fence post for support. The fire was moving into the underbrush, helped along by an increasing wind.

Meanwhile sirens of more units from Colorado City and Rye were screaming up the hill. Smoke plumes rose hundreds of feet above the ridge and could be seen fifty miles away. The road out in front of Clem's was getting congested. Neighbors and rubberneckers were stopping to help and watch. Out of the smoke came two imposing vehicles and they pulled into the field, a water tanker and fire engine. Behind them were several Pueblo County Sheriff 4x4's with emergency lights wildly flashing. The sheriffs at once blocked the road and set up a perimeter. Clem noticed Patsy's patrol car was one of them. They ordered all nonessential vehicles and persons to leave the area. The sheriff's department had already cordoned off the main town road to through traffic. Clem could overhear from the sheriff's radio that the Elementary and High School were on evacuation alert and a "return to work" call for all school bus drivers to assist with evacuation was issued. They were to transport some students to Craver Middle School in Colorado City some eight miles away. Others were to be deposited closer in Rye.

Clem slowly turned his head taking in all that was going on around him. If the days prior were simply a bad dream, today was the culmination of hell on earth. He saw flames lick the pine trees.

An abandoned backhoe near the top of the ridge had its tires flaming, pumping dark, black demonic clouds into an innocent sky. The fire had gotten too close and it could not be saved. The fuel line had melted and spewing out gallons of diesel fuel and igniting the ground beneath.

Suddenly there was a burst of sparks and a tremendous hissing sound. A large juniper with its volatile oily sap had exploded. For a moment all eyes were fixed on the erupting flames. All of the drought-stressed foliage transformed into a continuous blaze in the tinderbox conditions. Clem watched the firemen hose certain sections and hot spots with a high-powered fine spray. At times it appeared it would be over soon. Then the wind would stir and whip the flames into a frenzy.

*2:45 PM*

By now the fire had been burning for an hour or so. Water tender trucks holding 3000 gallons, able to release 1000 gallons a minute, rumbled into position. Smaller trucks holding 500 gallon each also roared into position near the base of the ridge. Other fire agency vehicles swung in to close any gaps. The plan of action was to surround and drown.

Clem was told he had to move out of the entrance way. He staggered towards the house and saw the dogs hunkered down underneath the porch both intently observing the mayhem. He knew they were frightened with the hellacious commotion and presence of fire. As he stepped onto the porch they whimpered and cringed between his legs. He mindlessly patted them and plopped down on a red steel folding chair. The dogs ran back under the porch.

The firefighters were scurrying up the hill on either side of the flames. Some were coming from the other side of the ridge and seemed to be yelling directions, but it was difficult to hear anything over the din of the firestorm. To the north of the ridge came a bulldozer. It had entered from Spencer's and was cutting a firebreak. The men hurried over the ridge and proceeded to hack away at underbrush on the far side of the firebreak.

As Clem looked on, he was trying to gauge how much had been destroyed so far. A great deal of his lower pasture was blackened. Five to ten acres of his neighbors on the southeast corner of the ridge was shimmering in flames. The fire was steadily progressing up the hill and to the southeast engulfing anything in its furious path.

Clem bowed his head and laid it in his palms and moaned. He smelt burnt flesh. He lifted his head and looked at his arms and hands, turning them over several times. All the hair was singed off and the skin was reddish and puffy. His pants were blackened with cinder burns up to his hips. His boots were solid gray-black, and the heels slightly melted. He reached up to push his hat back and whistled, but there was only air. His hat was gone.

Clem sat on the red chair motionless. His eyes were glassy and unresponsive. Shock had set in. With his arms and hands burning from the flames, he felt chilled but was incapable of moving. An ambulance was weaving through the crowd of vehicles. At the roadblock, a sheriff approached. The driver leaned out and inquired about any injuries. The sheriff pointed towards Clem then signaled it past. The driver pulled up in front of Clem's house. Two EMTs got out and removed medical response bags from the side door. They walked up to the porch. The dogs gave halfhearted barks but did not leave the under-porch. The EMTs introduced themselves. Clem stared off towards the fire. They asked if they could examine his hands and arms. Clem slowly turned and raised both arms. The EMTs evaluated his injuries. They told Clem he had first-degree burns on the top of his forearms, but that underneath he had second-degree burns. They explained that those areas would soon blister. Clem was compliant but silent. They removed his wristwatch and poured cool sterile water from a bottle over both arms, lightly daubed and dried them. Then they applied sterile gauze bandages, wrapping from hands to elbows. One of the EMTs slightly pinched the skin on Clem's neck and watched the skin react.

"This fella's dehydrated." He turned to his partner.

"Here," said his partner handing him the water jug and a paper cup.

"You need to drink this," the EMT said and lifted the cup to Clem's lips.

Clem looked up at the EMT and sipped.

"Can I have more?" Clem asked as he finished.

The EMT refilled the cup and Clem drank. He was beginning to snap out of his daze.

Above the din of sirens, air-horn blasts, engine roar, and yells from firefighters came a subsonic thumping and trembling of air. From the ridge above the treetops, a massive helicopter came to a hover. Then it released hundreds of gallons of water, which saturated the ground near the firebreak. After the release hatch was closed it veered off down behind the ridge and out of sight. The sound of the engine thumping and popping gradually faded. It was returning to Table Mountain, about three miles away to the east, to refill from a holding pond there.

The fire inched its way up the ridge spreading north and south. In the most imminent danger were Clem's neighbor to the south, Jason and Janet Galway. They'd been out of town for the past week visiting relatives in Phoenix. Their 35-acre property butted up against and above Clem's on the south-east side. It was their backhoe smoldering on the hillside. The fire department was using their driveway as an access to the upper ridge south of the fire.

Clem drank some more water. He stared in silence. The smoke was forming huge vortex columns reaching high into the sky. The fire's heat was causing its own wind. The smoke would spiral up and collide with upper wind currents and then disperse. At times the smoke made it impossible to see anything and then it would be pushed away by various breezes from off Cuerno Verde.

Most of the activity was concentrated on the south end of the ridge in order to minimize the fire's destructive path towards the houses below. The bulldozer had made its way to the center on the ridge continuing to cut a broad firebreak. Periodically great white streams of water would jet out from hoses wetting the area. Another tremendous rumble could be heard approaching. This time a Goliath-sized, orange helicopter appeared, hovered for a moment then dropped its load of slurry just to the north of the bulldozer and fire crews. Before the slurry hit the ground, the helicopter had roared away . . .

. . . Light little puffs of cottonwood slowly drifted down from above. Clem watched them eddy in the atmosphere. Miniature clouds fell silently in a gentle sway. Clem felt himself sway, the sway of a boat. His eyes closed, and he swayed, as he had in Rainey's arms during hot summer nights. Silently, as breaths in darkness. He swayed gently and opened his eyes. The little light puffs were still falling and landing on his nose and eyelids. "This isn't cottonwood," he grumbled, "it's ash."

The EMT eyed him cautiously, "How you doing?"

"It's ash."

"Yeah, how 'bout that?"

"Holy Shit."

"You can say that again."

Clem looked at the EMT. His look was hollow; a dried hollow, skull look.

"How you doing?" She asked again, observing him.

"Holy Shit!"

The EMT gave a hushed laugh through her nose. She handed him a water cup and as he drank she felt his forehead with the back of her hand, holding it there as she looked around at the explosive scene. She and her partner probably would be here for the better part of the afternoon and into the evening. There was also the likelihood of having to transport the old man too. Keep him overnight for observation. Standard operating procedures. It had all the earmarks of a busy time ahead.

Clem squeezed and crinkled the empty water cup. The sound brought back the attention of the EMT. She told Clem that they should take him to the emergency room for further treatment. Clem balked at the thought of leaving, "Nix on that honey. I'm sticking around here until it's out!" She conveyed her present assessment, "It doesn't appear that you're in shock, but you're disoriented, exhausted, dehydrated, and have first and second-degree burns on your hands and arms. I strongly advise that you to go to the emergency room."

"Yeah, yeah. As soon as they put the kibosh on this here fire," Clem insisted.

"OK, I can't force you. But we'll be here for some time and keep an eye on your condition," she said and handed him another paper cup of water.

"That's a good girl," Clem said, back to his old self.

The EMT gave him a look.

The vicinity roared with helicopters, fire trucks, sirens and yells from various emergency crews. Most of the activity was concentrated on the ridge southeast of where the fire had originated.

*3:20 PM*

On the ridge-top the small bulldozer inched along cutting a path in the parched earth. Fire crews followed, hacking away at the underbrush and low-lying branches. The fire-resistant Ponderosa pine bark would stand up against the flames. All were hedging their bets that the fire would simply extinguish itself for lack of fuel.

During this time the elementary and high schools were in full evacuation procedures. School buses were dropping off children in front of the Methodist Church on the corner of Hwy 165 and Main Street. Parents jammed the parking lot. Cars zigzagged in front of buses making the unloading of children hazardous. Once a bus stopped it could not move due to the traffic jam, which caused the other buses to hold children until they could proceed to a safe drop-off point. This in turn caused a bottleneck at the entrance to the town itself.

Just across Highway 165 opposite the Church, was the high school. It now housed the Command Center for all the various emergency crews, fire departments and law enforcement agencies. News networks with cameramen and broadcasters began arriving. They maneuvered their vans into neat rows with satellite dishes protruding from their roofs. Film crews were busy capturing all the events for the evening news at five.

Further down the highway about eight miles the Red Cross was preparing quarters to house evacuees at the Craver Middle School gymnasium. Contingencies for medical supplies, cots, water and food were being discussed by volunteers and staff in the event of a worse-case scenario.

At the same time as the Red Cross arrival, Craver was dismissing its students for the day. Worried parents arrived to shuttle their loved ones home, at the same time school buses pulled up to unload and load students. General confusion abounded with parents and children scurrying about, a nightmare in the works for bus drivers, teachers and the principal.

*3:45 PM*

As the afternoon wore on, the town grew darker and darker as the valley filled with smoke. An eerie orange glow above Rattlesnake Ridge had all eyes upon it. Lookie-loo's were capturing pictures with their cell phones and others were calling loved ones. Word was out that the Fire Chief had publicly categorized the fire as a Type 3 fire, the categories being 1 through 5 with 1 being the worst. This was a serious fire based on its locale to this community with multiple structures and the potential loss of life. With the fire's progression, officials ordered roads closed in the immediate vicinity and recommended evacuation of the 250 residents in town. Rye residents that chose to leave could find shelter at the Middle School.

Highway 165 was now closed to all through traffic. Only emergency vehicles were allowed to pass.

The stink of panic began to drift down polluting the town of Rye. As the smoky haze thickened around the houses and streets, residents — those that were able to get to their homes — prepared to evacuate. These townsfolk hurried about loading their cars with vital papers and valuables, pets and clothing. It would be a long night for many residents.

*4:30 PM*

Still on the red, steel, folding chair, Clem sat in awe at the spectacle of machinery and manpower that was unleashed on what had been a little grass fire. Helicopters thundered and spewed their water and slurry. Bulldozers ripped and tore the land. Men savagely hacked at the brush clearing the way and others furiously sprayed with their hoses. Flames rippled off the tops of pines extending hundreds of feet into the gray-brown sky. Smoldering acreage lay blackened from the onslaught of flames. All of it was out of his control. He was a spectator, a very important spectator. He had created this beast; this infant had grown to be a monster. He was at the heart of it. This is what he had desperately tried to ignore at the very instant he heard that sound, a summary of a lifetime of consequences too terrible to comprehend. Now he lay in the smoldering acreage of those decisions with metallic screams echoing in his mind.

*5:00 PM*

The entire ridge-top glowed an eerie redish-orange. White smoke shot out at different points when pockets of pine or juniper sap explode. Some of the fire crew had to step back away from their work due to the intense heat.

*5:45 PM*

At this point the path of the fire no longer progressed. It was halted at the ridge-top with the firebreak on the east side and the already consumed acreage to the west. The fire was living on borrowed time, burning up what remained of brush and limbs. In this precarious lull fire crews knew better than to slacken their efforts. The situation was fraught with unpredictable elements. Winds could build or hot spots might erupt. Sparks or embers could ignite anywhere they landed in the arid conditions. All were secretly hoping for a lucky break.

From the cab of the fire truck, command dispatch reports could be overheard from the radio. Clem was within earshot and listening intently to updates and progress. There was a call for one more drop to be made by the helicopter on the east side of the firebreak. Orders were also given to retrace steps to quell any areas that might harbor any material still burning. Clem felt these were encouraging signs and that things might be winding down. He looked at the paper cup in his hand and swirled the remaining liquid around. He stared at the clear vortex and thought of various religious images. He wanted to pray or ask for forgiveness or thank someone or something. Only fragments of past prayers came to mind. He could start but finish none that he began. He tangled them together in a strange spiritual quagmire of grace.

*6:15 PM*

Clem leaned forward, elbows to knees and one of the dogs suddenly came up and nosed his hand. The paper cup jolted and jettisoned the remaining water into Clem's face. Clem shuttered and inhaled a quick breath and snapped out of his reverence. The cool moisture felt good. The dog nosed in and licked his face. He patted the dog's head with his hand wrapped in gauze. He realized his hands and arms hurt. In fact, he hurt all over. His back and rear were stiff from sitting on the hard, red chair. He had been there, petrified, for some time. He cast his grim gaze at the ridge and whispered, "Come on and die, damn it!" Then he looked at the sheriff's deputies standing by the road. They seemed to be chatting and paying no attention to the activities on the ridge. Perhaps they sensed the situation easing up or had secret knowledge that this was a done deal, or, they were simply bored. He saw the paramedics near the fire Chief's truck all pointing towards the ridge and talking. He looked up when the helicopter appeared in the distance and dropped its load of water. Both dogs were wagging their stubs in front of him almost as if they were about to say something. Clem knew they were scared. There hadn't been this much excitement on the ranch ever. He groaned when he rose from the chair and stood there on the porch, lightheaded, and tried to stretch. "Jesus," he said, turned and entered the house with the dogs squeezing in behind.

In the kitchen he filled the water bowls then went to the pantry and tried to grab the bag of dry dog food. It slipped from his grip. "Shit," he griped. Filling both bowls he dropped the bag with a thump leaving it sitting in the middle of the kitchen. The dogs wagged and scarfed up the meal. He listened to the munching sounds and wobbled back and forth. Then the phone rang. It kept ringing and he kept ignoring it. It rang and rang, and he forgot it. He turned and stood at the sink counter and leaned towards the window. In the glass he saw his reflection with the backdrop of flames and smoke everywhere. He shook his head from side to side then there was a knock at the front door. He walked slowly through the living room catching his boot heel on the edge of the rug, stumbling. He regained his balance reaching the front screen in a huff.

One of the paramedics called in. "How you doing?"

"I'm burnt to shit and hurt like a son of a bitch. Other than that, swell," Clem said.

"That's great!"

"What? That I'm burnt to shit or hurt like hell?"

"Both, that's how we gauge that your cognizant and functioning. Otherwise we'd probably have to transport you to the ER."

"I think I'll get along."

"You're gonna want to keep those dressings changed and cleaned. And get on some antibiotics right away to avoid infection."

"I'll give my doc a holler in the morning."

"Hope you have plenty of extra strength Tylenol. You're gonna need it!"

"I'm good, thanks for all your help."

"We'll be around for while if you need anything, OK?"

"Yeah, OK." he said.

It dawned on Clem that he'd been talking to the paramedic through the screen door, never opening it, as if trying to keep out the world. He certainly wished he could keep the world out now. But all hell was going to want to find out how this fire started.

The phone began ringing again.

He began ignoring it again.

He turned and went to the kitchen and gave a sharp whistled through his teeth and the dogs bolted up. He swung the back door open and hissed, "Git!" They zoomed by and Clem followed walking to the back pasture and whistling for the Appaloosa. He could see its head just above the back knoll. It wasn't going to come. Clem smirked. He didn't blame it. *I wouldn't come either*, he thought.

The yellow field glowed and shimmered like a shower of golden topaz. The sun hung in a red veil, like a mistress from hell. Clem clenched his stinging fists and turned back towards the house. He rounded the east side where he'd abandoned his tractor. A leaden sadness, gray and heavy, came over him, slowing his pace. Looking up, it appeared there was less commotion on the ridge. Most of the flames had diminished. As he approached the unit chief's truck, he heard declaration coming from the cab that the fire was 80% contained. This should have elicited joy but instead he veered off and continued toward the front porch. The deputies had pulled their vehicles to the side of the road, but the emergency lights were still flashing. Clem stepped up on the porch and patted his shirt pocket for smokes. He hadn't had a cigarette since, well . . . he couldn't recall. Filching one from the pack he tried to envision the moments leading up to the grinding sound when the tractor jumped. With the cigarette stuck to his dry lips his bandaged hands felt for matches. With difficulty he managed, with two fingers, to slide the pack from his hip pocket. Swiping the sulfur tip on the strike pad he brought the flame close. His hands shook. The cigarette wavered and he dragged hard. A fume billowed from his lips then he spit. Scary thoughts flashed like careening cars coming head on at him. He stared at the black spot where the rock was. Where the sound had been. He blinked and held his stare. A ringing began and rose in volume. He ignored it, or at least tried.

*7:00 PM*

From the porch Clem could see that some fire personnel were retracting hoses, cleaning and securing them. The bulldozer had completed digging the perimeter and was disappearing back down the northeast side of the ridge. The two slurry bombers from Jefferson County had been called off. Smaller more maneuverable fire trucks were driving up the blackened hillside stopping periodically to douse a smoldering tree stump or shrub. One of the Deputies' 4x4s pulled away and drove off down the road.

Clem watched the fire unit chief heading in his direction. Jay Hickman, Unit Chief of the Colorado City Fire Department, was of medium build and height with short cropped hair and a thin mustache. Determined light blue eyes zeroed in on Clem as he approached with a clipboard in hand. Clem dropped his cigarette on the porch and toed it out.

"How's it going?" Clem asked.

"Well right now we have the upper hand. Winds are calm and containment is near complete, although you never know. Fires can never be underestimated."

Clem nodded without a word.

"We'll most likely be here for most of the night, at least a unit or two, to observe and keep an eye on things." He paused before continuing. "Mr. Everett, the preliminary report I have regarding the cause of the fire is a spark from the tractor over there," gesturing in the tractor's direction. "Is that right?"

"Well yeah, think I hit a boulder or something. You know how it is tall grass and all."

"Uh huh. This is just routine." Jay scribbled notes on his clipboard. "About what time did you observe the fire?"

Clem was about to scratch his forehead but stopped because his hand ached. "Not quite sure. Somewheres around two o'clock, I reckon."

"Another fire official from the Forest Service will contact you most likely tomorrow when things are not so hectic. The department is required to file a report that will be reviewed. There will also be a Sheriff present because this is County."

Clem nodded without a word.

"They will require a more detailed report and will do preliminary analysis of the incident." Jay jotted away as he spoke. "You sustained some injuries I see," looking at Clem's bandaged hands.

"Thought I could put the damn thing out." He said.

Jay paused and nodded. He took a slow look at Clem then said, "Keep those burns clean and get on some antibiotics. Well, that's all for now. Someone will be by tomorrow Mr. Everett. Take it easy." Jay walked back to his truck where other personnel were gathering.

The sky was clearing and the men on the hillside were less frantic. The roar of commotion had softened. The night was tiptoeing-in as usual like nobody's business. A crescent moon peekabooed in and out of the fading smoke. It was watching Clem before Clem spied it. "I thought it'd never end," he whispered. This whole day was merely nothing in the sneaky rotation of the planets. Clem really sensed that. He was feeling small and puny.

He went for his hat and it was not there.

He went for his cigarette and the pack was empty.

He spat a dry nothing.

Looking at the front yard torn up from truck tires he bit his lip. He watched the paramedics get in their truck, back out and drive off. The chill of a cold loneliness came over him, a loneliness of self-accusation. He began to dread the idea of going into the house. He had had enough of soul-searching and wretched self-doubt. He shivered and stepped off the porch deciding to look for his hat. When he got to where he thought he lost it the ground was solid black. He kicked the thick wet soot. There was the boulder he hit. He let his eyes wander; his hat was not there. He turned to go back to the house and did not look to see if anyone was watching him. As he stepped from the charred ground and moved into the yellow grass, he spotted it, his hat, singed and streaked with charcoal. He bent over and picked it up, lightly slapping it against his trousers then tweaked it to straighten the brim. He slowly placed it upon his head and continued back to the house. He was trying to be dignified. He knew it was absurd. Dayglo white bandages on both hands, hat slightly crushed, filthy black soot-all-over clothes and a gait that was anything but dignified.

Reaching the backside of the house Clem veered off towards the upper pasture. The horse had to be corralled for the night. He lifted the halter off the gate where he had left it earlier. Flipping the latch, he swung open the gate and whistled for the Appaloosa. Off by the knoll it flicked its tail and raised its head in Clem's direction. He whistled again. The horse shook its mane and sauntered towards Clem.

He waited.

The horse took its time.

As he watched the horse the pit of his stomach churned. The picture he saw was that of a dream he had had for many years. A beautiful Appaloosa roaming a lush field. His field. His Appaloosa. Tears rolled along his sooty cheeks making watery channels on pale flesh. His chest heaved in an autonomic quiver taking in three short breaths. He knew this was it. All it was ever going to be. The horse now stood placidly in front of Clem and snorted. Clem stood there, shoulders drooping, a washed-out scarecrow after a downpour, the straw of life falling about his tattered existence. He put his hand on the horse's rump and touched the spots walking his fingers one to the other. The spots became galaxies of regret. One irregular shaped failure after the next. More tears channeled down his face painting a forest of prison bars and he was trapped there behind those bars of tears.

*8:00 PM*

Clem led the horse into the corral, unclipped the halter and closed the gate behind him. Then he walked directly into the house and to the bathroom. He dropped his hat on the toilet seat. With effort he put the drain plug in the sink and filled the sink halfway with cold water. He dipped a washcloth with his fingers and clumsily wiped his face doing his darndest to keep the gauze from getting wet. He repeated the process several times until he could recognize himself in the mirror. He then used the washcloth to clean his hat. Afterwards it looked more white than black, he called it good and pulled the plug letting the scummy gray water drain. He put his hat back on and walked to the front door. As he passed the phone in the hallway it rang. At the sound of it his knees buckled slightly, and he stopped. This time he picked up the receiver and said "Yeah."

"Clem, is that you?" the voice asked.

"Yep! Who's this?"

"Janet Galway."

Clem hardened and answered, "Oh hey, how ya doing?"

"Clem, are you all right?"

"Yeah, just a little nuts around here."

"We are in Phoenix and got a call about a fire."

"Yeah, well the damnedest thing happened."

"The news on the television mentioned that nineteen acres was burned."

"Yeah . . . Your place is OK. It never got that far."

"Some friends called and informed us about that already. I was concerned about *you*."

"I'm fine. Just kinda busy at the moment."

"Clem, I won't keep you, we'll be back late tomorrow if there is anything you need."

"OK, thanks for the call."

"Clem, I mean it, just let us know."

"OK, thanks."

Clem was relieved to hang up the phone. No details to explain. He was not quite honest about his answers. The Galways had lost a tractor and good portion of pine on the west side of their 35 acres. He mumbled, "It could have been worse."

At the front door he swung open the screen and peered out without stepping onto the porch. Both heelers were there, stubs wagging, looking up at him. He shoved the screen wider and let them in. He then stepped out to have a look-see. The only vehicles remaining were a sheriff's 4x4 in the road, the structural truck that had first arrived, a water tanker and a smaller fire engine that was roaming the hillside. Fire personnel on foot were still poking around the slope with shovels for hot spots. He could not see any visible flames. He flipped his wrist up to take a gander at his wristwatch and at the same time remembered the EMT had removed it. It was in his trouser's front pocket. He stuck two fingers in and managed to manipulate it out. It looked like he was doing the hula. He glanced at it.

*8:10 PM*

Clem knew he could be of no use out there, "If they need somethin' they'll come get me," he mumbled to himself. He went back inside. He took care of the dogs and horse but neglected himself. He knew he was tired and famished, but part of him couldn't think of eating. He felt better fidgeting and pacing when he was nervous. His quest was cigarettes and maybe a shot of something. The carton of Marlboro's was on the counter. He rattled the carton and a pack popped out. He went through the ritual of packing the pack of cigarettes against his thigh a few times but gave up, due to the pain it caused in his hands. His hands ached. He peeled the cellophane off and folded the top back and popped up a few. He lifted the pack to his mouth and lipped one out. He did the hula again to get the pack of matches out of his pants. It was all a fantastic ordeal.

In the cupboard above the sink was bottle of J&B. He reached up and pulled it down, at the same time fingering a glass in the sink. He shuffled to the kitchen table and fell into the chair. He unscrewed the cap, filled the glass half full, screwed the cap back on and placed the bottle next to the glass, the cigarette hanging from his lips the whole time. He ashed it, then took a deep drag and put it in the ashtray. Picking up the glass he paused, made and O with his lips blowing a smoke ring at the glass. He watched the ring collide with the glass and dissolve, then he finally swallowed its contents. The whiskey made him grimace. It felt warm in his mouth and down his throat. It made him tingle. His empty stomach immediately began to absorb the alcohol. It was on rarer and rarer occasion that he drank. Not that he drank that much to begin with. He didn't like people when they drank. Most of them showed their second face. Maybe it was his second face he didn't want to show. In any case the J&B had been neglected and wore a dust overcoat. The last time was when he and Rainey toasted a New Year's right here in this kitchen. They got just a little tipsy and Rainey had started to dance. Clem, without thinking, slid into her arms and led her around in a two-step. It was the only step Clem could do. There was no music, just Rainey humming a strange lilt. It didn't matter they were entwined in a brief romantic kitchen promenade; it had lasted in Clem's mind for years.

Clem took a drag from his cigarette and poured another half-glass. "Here's to you sweetie." He raised the glass slightly. He and Rainey had been over now for some time, but he was used to talking to her this way. He didn't mind, he liked having his own personal *Pooka*. He held the toast as if he were waiting for her to clink glasses. In this momentary repose a tiny waft of smoke came from his nostrils. Pantomiming the clink, he drank. He swallowed hard and coughed. Then he rose quickly, pushing the chair over accidentally. He put the glass on the table and walked to the hallway and took the phone off the cradle. He was protecting his phantasmagoric instant. The whiskey helped him believe that, but his gut knew it was shit. He was hightailing it for safety. There would be lots of explaining to do tomorrow. Tonight, he had to get his story straight, get his wits about him. He needed to avoid interruptions.

Back in the kitchen he picked up the chair. He still ached. He opened one of the kitchen drawers and rummaged around for a bottle of Tylenol. Struggling with the safety cap he managed to shake out two 500 milligrams tablets. He left the bottle on the counter and went back to the table. He tossed the tablets in his mouth and poured a short shot and slugged it down. He stood there sagging, alone. Then that pleasant feeling started creeping up, when the world seems golden and you are a physical masterpiece. Clem's eyelids drooped and he relished the brief euphoria. "It will be OK," he wished. He worked that wish for a few minutes more, and then the buzz was fading.

Clem looked up at the clock on the wall. It read 9:30. He smiled and stared at the clock. He and Rainey had picked it up at the souvenir shop on Main Street at Disneyland, a stupid little electric clock of Disney's Goofy with his arms as the minute and hour hands, his puffy white gloves pointing to the time. Clem had looked at the clock a thousand casual times. This time, time stood still. There they were, he and Rainey in the shop surrounded by hundreds of fragile glass figurines and pixies, glistening in happiness.

Clem fixated on Goofy's second hand as it bobbed on three. Then it dropped to five and continued on its merry way. It was an old clock now. He looked out the window and could only see the clearance lights on two trucks parked at the base of the hill. Time ticked away. He had made it through this day.

# Five
## Friday, 13th

*The thing's leg appeared from the hallway. It was red and blue with barnacles growing on it. Then another one, mechanically out of sync with the other, jittering spasmodically quick. The thorny bulbous body came next, spotted like a bloated horned toad. The thing crawled sideways and when it turned at the corner of the bedroom doorway its full grotesquery was revealed. Chilling cries came from the face. It was the face of Comanche Chief Tabivo Naritgant. Its head protruded from the spiked torso and it called to Clem, "Come closer, it is time." The headdress transformed into gorgon-slithering reptiles. It then unfurled a scorpion's tail with an immense stinger dripping a yellow-green pus. It came for him . . .*

Clem's eyes were twitching rapidly under the lids . . . *He was trying to run but couldn't get his footing. He would fall, get up and then get tangled in a bush, get free and fall again in the loose rocks. The sheets copied his twitching feet underneath. From an open window the silent air drove in and cruised the room. The curtains lifted and fell, lifted and fell. The thing was closing in and Clem could do nothing to stop it.*

With a gasp Clem opened his eyes. It took him a few seconds to get his bearings and to know it was a dream. "A goddamn nightmare." His mouth dry and heart pounding, he lay there while beads of sweat swan dived onto the pillow. The curtain lifted and fell, lifted and fell. The silent air whispered, "I'm here," and landed on him, cooling his forehead.

Clem orbited his eyes towards the nightstand. The hands and hours of Big Ben were still illuminated. He had only been asleep for an hour. He noticed a low hum from one of the fire engines. His eyes inspected each object on the nightstand then halted on the jar with the arrowhead and shard. Clem wasn't especially a memorabilia sort of guy. The things he did keep he kept in boxes and drawers and never looked at them. He'd been down that road. Most of the things had secrets in them. To the casual observer the things appeared simply as junk, but the stuff hidden inside usually made him emotional, so he left most of those things alone. The shard was different though.

Clem and Rainey had found it together. They were hiking one afternoon around the foothills of Madrid, New Mexico. Madrid was a mining town on the Turquoise Trail. In the sixties, hippie squatters invaded and took up residence. Now it boasted art galleries and gift shops for tourists. Rainey had suggested they ride out there. So, still in the throes of newfound love, where everything was possible again, they set out on their little jaunt. It was in the fall. By late afternoon the low desert sun was streaming rays easterly across the Chamisa, casting long deep shadows. It made the yellow flowers seem brilliant.

As they meandered along the path, they came upon a huge bull snake stretched out, sunning itself. Clem was about to heave a rock at it, but Rainey stopped him. She told him the snake was a good omen. Bull snakes are old spirits of the earth. They were there to help us pay attention to Mother Nature. Of course, Clem thought otherwise. He remembered the biblical story of the devil taking the form of a snake and tempting Adam and Eve in the garden of paradise. Hell, everybody he knew killed the damn things. This woman sure was different. A good omen was a good omen, he figured, and so he dropped the rock and the snake slid out of sight into the underbrush. They both watched it and when the tip of its tail disappeared, they noticed something in the smooth of the sand. Something almost the same color of the snake but man-made. Rainey reached down and dusted it off with her fingertip, then picked it up. The object was a small piece of pottery, triangular in shape, two inches long and about a quarter inch thick. Line designs were painted on it in tans, burnt umber and reds. She

119

handed it to Clem, and they walked on. She told him the shard was probably made by Pueblo Indians from 300 to about 1000 years ago. And that during burial ceremonies it was customary to break pottery jars or bowls and bury them along with the dead. Clem listened to Rainey talk in her husky tones and kept feeling the shard in his pocket. Sometimes he rubbed it against his hip like some Aladdin's lamp hoping to get three wishes out of the day.

They walked and talked while the sun set and a full moon rose. They stopped at some ruined mining shacks above the town. The moon shown through the broken windows and warped boards of the tilting abandoned buildings. They watched bats flicker in the dusk air. It was a setting for Wild West ghost stories, and they kissed under broken eaves and splintered moon rays. Clem thought her magical and had wanted something magical in his life. On they kissed while the moon rays danced on their skin . . .

Clem closed his eyes and envisioned one of those moon rays and tried to ride it back to sleep. The curtains lifted and fell, lifted and fell. Outside the night was clear and warm. The hillside was black with several faint ghostlike spirals that rose into the night. A few firefighters were clustered next to the vehicle drinking coffee from thermoses. You could just barely hear snippets of laughter. The faces and gestures of the men were highlighted by the red strobe light on top of the truck. The truck's communications radio was still turned up so that periodically it sent out piercing updates from the command post at Rye High School. By now evacuations orders had been rescinded and most of the town's residents had returned to their homes.

Clem faded in and out of consciousness to the backdrop of sounds emanating from the lower field. He tossed and turned based on his perceived pain levels. He woke and dozed to the intensity of each nightmare. The combination of pain, noise, alcohol, Tylenol, worry, heat and an empty stomach made delectable fuel for the mind to wreak havoc on one's dreamscape. Every time he realized his eyes were open, he would moan, "This is gonna be a long night." He said it so many times that it became part of each half-dream or trance he was in at the time.

As the night tottered on, his hallucinations grew bolder. Clem's R.E.M activity maxed out during one whopper of a dream.

*In the dream, he was a young boy running down the street where he lived. As the street became more and more steep, he extended his arms bird-like and somehow took flight. The sensation of altitude thrilled him, and he willed himself even higher. As he soared over the neighborhood, he somehow managed to ascend and descend with great agility and acceleration. After what seemed like forever in dreamtime he returned to his street and landed near his home. He ran inside his house searching for someone to tell of his exploits. He ran from room to room opening the doors. Each room looked out onto a wondrous yellow field. He finally came to the last door and opened it slowly. It was his room when he was twelve years old. Everything was there, bedspread with images of cowboys on it, his baseball glove, comic books and model cars, his shoes and favorite jacket, books on mechanics and his pet hamster. The room smelled the same too. It was as real as could be, so he went to the bed and bounced on it like old times then sat a moment and dangled his feet over the edge wiggling his toes. Where did my shoes go? He stopped moving and waited in silence. He was then compelled to walk to the closet and open it. Placing his hand on the knob he shuddered and tried to pull away. His hand was stuck to it like a tongue to an ice tray in the freezer. He knew if he pulled too hard all his fingerprints would be irretrievably left on the knob for eternity. His only solution was to turn the knob and open the door. He did so with the greatest of effort. He had to pull very hard at the heavy door. As it opened, all the air from the room was sucked into the closet. A horrible wind roared past Clem. He could not get air in his lungs but could not release the knob either. He tugged with all his might and, when the door was finally wide open, his hand gave way. He peered into the darkness of the closet. He moved in closer for a better look. Something was slowly swinging in the closet's twilight. He moved in even closer. His lungs were about to burst, and he looked hard and squinted. It was a little boy. Clem took another step. He could not feel his lungs any longer. He stared at the boy. The harder he stared the more the boy looked like him. It was him, not the troubled boy, but Clem hanging there by the neck from an extension cord tied to a clothes hook.*

*Clem turned and ran.*

*His feet and legs swished along in tall yellow stems. He was in the yellow field running, running as fast as he could. He needed air. He knew he was running but at the same time saw himself running from above like two dreams at once and the only sound was the grass swishing against his pants. Looking up at the bright blue sky he opened his mouth and . . .*

He woke, this time buckling forward on the bed and gasping for breath. He panted awhile. The air moved around him cautiously. The curtain was falling and settled still. The moon had arced to the west and now beamed into Clem's bedroom. Its glow illuminated the white sheets and gauze bandages on Clem's hands. Big Ben ticked behind him. He cocked his head and glanced at the time. 4:50 a.m. He turned back around and looked at his hands.

*This is the start of my punishment and penance he began thinking*, a train of thought that hadn't visited his station since he was a teenager. The caboose of strict indoctrination was never unhooked and had tagged along regardless of his denials and influences. Choices and consequences, snakes and omens, confusion and sanity, belief and disbelief alternately ticked along with Big Ben in Clem's mind. He wondered if he'd allowed himself to fall for that fire and brimstone shit for a convenient solution to his choices or dig in and see it for the simple cause-and-effect that it all seemed to be. He saw clearly how his weariness and pain were looking for an easy scapegoat. How human beings get weathered and beat down day after day, especially when they are not mindful. How being mindful gets lost in so much living packed into such a small vessel overlapping and mixing and bursting at the seams and can sometimes be more than a human can sustain. *Is how you live your life here on earth some heaven and hell of your own manifestation? Is life such an unsolvable question that the ultimate answer is god? Is god the thumb in the dike holding back the lake of unknowns?*

It was dawning on Clem that his proverbial shit was hitting the fan and he wondered if he'd be around to see where it all landed. The right time and place seemed to apply not only to fame and fortune, but also to failure and anonymity. *Or maybe,* he thought, *the right attitude could be attached to the wrong goal and lead you down the path you least expected. Sometimes all you are from birth to the grave may add up to zero if you don't let the numbers count. Who the hell is counting, and what's it all count for?* He could work these angles all night but still not find any tidy box to put it all in.

The curtain rose softly and caught Clem's eye. He was eyeball-to-eyeball with the moon for a second and then he blinked. I need some more shuteye, he reckoned, and eased back onto his bed of thorns. He began to get an old strange feeling that his hands were gigantic, close to his face, an inside-mother's-womb visual with your hands and feet so close, so huge, so singular and present, so individually important, so first-experiential a sensation. He knew it was all coming down to the million-dollar question of meaning. As he took a deep breath, the breath stuttered before the cry. The cry did not come. He cinched it off quick, but an errant tear escaped and hesitantly crept along one of his many channeled crowsfeet. He blew out the breath. It rose in the room, into the pool of air above him and pirouetted and skimmed past the moonbeams at the windowsill then rioted in the fall night and was gone. He slept.

As Clem stirred from his slumber, there was that euphoric period. A brief moment before one succumbs to reality where the body is free of pain, the mind is between worlds, a tender moment of innocence hovers, and then the first struggle of regret and one wakes. Clem opened his eyes. The room was torturously bright. He had missed the morning. The clothes he still wore were soaked with sweat. He could smell himself. He sat up. The sheets were smudged with soot. The pillow was on the floor beside the bed. The curtains stood still. A solo fly flew patterns of squares near the window. Another fly buzzed, wiggling in a web at the corner of the screen. Clem felt his hangover in the chunks of lead hanging at the base of his skull.

Without thinking anymore, he went to the bathroom and made a bath of cold water. He stripped and dipped his toe in. The coolness helped melt the lead hangover. He squatted down in the cold water constantly catching his breath, moaning, "Ooh, ooh, ooh." He fingered a washcloth and dipped it in the water, rubbed the soap bar and washed bit by bit. The *ooh, ooh* lasted until he stepped out of the tub and left the mucky water behind. He dried, wrapping the towel around his waist and then shaved at the sink. The razor blade scraped and scratched at the stubs, stiff with the cold water. Then he rummaged in the hamper for clothes. After fighting with his shirtsleeves to get past the bandages, he found his boots and hat. He almost felt whole.

Downstairs was quiet. He went to the kitchen. "First things first," he said as he reached the table where he had left his cigarettes. He lit and dragged, stood there and listened. He couldn't remember if he had let the dogs in or out last night, but then decided that it was a certainty they weren't in or they'd be bustling in front of him now. He took a peek out the kitchen window. He saw one truck was near the base of the hill and two men were on the ridge. There were no signs of smoke that he could see.

"That's good," he said out loud. He cleared his throat and then the table, put the bottle of J&B back into the cupboard and made a quick cup of coffee. Sitting at the table he smoked and sipped his coffee trying to get a grip on the day. He figured on getting a few chores out of the way and seeing about his hands. He downed the last of the coffee, snubbed the butt out and walked to the hall. The receiver was still off the hook. He put it back on the cradle and picked up the phone book walking back to the kitchen. He checked the Goofy clock. It was 9:15 AM. Back in the hall he dialed the medical center in Colorado City and waited. The receptionist came on the line.

"Dr. Gibson's Office."

"Hey there, this Clem Everett and I was wondering if I could get in and see the doc this morning?"

"What seems to be the problem?"

"Had a little accident and burnt my hands." He knew she knew. It wasn't like it wasn't on the news all day yesterday. Hell, the whole state knew. It sure wasn't a secret he could keep.

"Hold just a moment, please." The line went to muzak and Clem rolled his eyes. He waited and listened.

"Mr. Everett?" her voice returned.

"Yeah, I'm still here."

"There was a cancellation and we can get you in after lunch at 1:20."

"That'll be just fine."

"Bring any insurance information if things have changed so we can update our files."

"Yeah, OK," he answered and then hung up.

Nothing had changed.

He didn't have any insurance.

He'd just pay up front and be done with it. It couldn't be that much, a little salve and a prescription for antibiotics and call it good. Maybe they'd give him the senior citizens discount rate or something.

At the back door, he gave a whistle for the dogs. They came running around the side of the house and scooted in past him. The screen door banged shut and Clem went for the bag of dog food. He poured kibble into each bowl. The dogs sat and watched with their heads slightly cocked. He fumbled several times, spilling kibble every which-way. "Come on." He said and motioned for them to eat. In a flash they were at the bowls. He returned the bag with a thump on the floor then looked at his hands. They were red and swollen. He put it out of his mind and then the phone rang. "Shit" he hissed.

"Hello," he answered.

"Yes, Mr. Everett, please?"

"That's me." His stomach knotted.

"Good morning, this is Sheriff Dayton Hays of Pueblo County. How are you this morning?"

"Chipper as a chipmunk in a pine tree. What can I do for you?" As if he didn't know.

"Well Mr. Everett this pertains to the fire that occurred yesterday on your property. We have a routine report to be completed and have a few questions. We need to meet with you sometime today. Is there a convenient time this afternoon that would work?

"Well it's kind of a nut house around here. There's about million things I gotta do. Have this doctor's appointment at 1:20. My hands got burnt up pretty bad…

"Would 3 o'clock work?' Dayton cut in.

Clem could tell by the sheriff's tone that 3 o'clock would have to work.

"Yeah I should be back. Probably have to pick up a prescription too."

"The report is a formality and shouldn't take that long. Chief Hickman of the Colorado City fire department will also be present."

"Yeah I met him yesterday."

"Right. See you at three, Mr. Everett."

"I'll be here." He let the receiver drop in the cradle. He did his dry lip-spit thing leaning against the wall. He knew this was coming. He shouldered off the wall, grabbed the pack of cigarettes from the table and marched out the back door heading for the corral.

The Appaloosa was standing in the sun swinging its tail from side to side shushing flies from its haunches. Clem entered the corral and walked into the barn for feed. From a bag he dumped a small pile of grain in the feed trough and checked the water in the tub near the entrance. It was low so he pulled a hose over and dropped the hose nozzle in. He went to the hydrant, lifted the handle, filled the tub three quarters full and pushed the handle back down. That would keep the mare for the day. The mare lifted her head as Clem closed the gate behind him. He stood there then lit another cigarette and looked at all the black ground. He lip-spit in disgust and walked to the tractor.

The tractor was where he left it, resting at the northwest corner of the lower field. The key was still in the ignition. The swather was still engaged. He put the cigarette in his mouth and struggled up on the steel seat. The steel was blistering hot and he hopped up taking the cigarette out of his mouth. "God damn," he hissed. He sat back down a few times letting his ass adjust to the heat. He'd broken a sweat now and wiped his brow with the dirty gauze on his hand. He started the engine, let it idle and took a drag. He blew the smoke out and then engaged the hydraulic and raised the swather. He put the tractor in gear. It sputtered and lurched forward. He drove it out the entrance gate and up to the shed next to the barn. He parked parallel to the bailer, lowered the swather until it rested on the ground and killed the engine. Getting off the machine was just as hard as getting on. He dropped his cigarette in the dirt, toed it, blew smoke out and looked around. He began to feel lightheaded and had to grab hold of the fender. The dizziness faded after a moment and Clem suspected he was weak due to not eating much in the last day or so. Little Debbie's and coffee just wasn't enough. He decided he'd gotten off to a pretty good start for the day and into the house he went.

In the kitchen, Clem rustled up a couple of sunny-side-up eggs, buttered toast and another cup of coffee. He broke open the tops of the yolks and daubed them with the toast. The butter and yolk dribbled onto his fingers and he quickly licked them clean. There was no sense in getting it all over the bandages, he figured. Plus, the blisters were forming and keeping them clean was probably wise. He was definitely trying to utilize some of his wisdom today. *Batten down the hatches before the storm, and all that stuff,* he thought.

Clem finished his meal and put the dishes in the sink, telling himself that he'd wash them later after dinner. Then he went to finish the laundry. He picked up the other half of the whites and shoved them in the washer. He tossed in a cup worth of detergent and set the washer cycle, pushed the knob and let the lid drop. As he put the box of detergent back, he realized how major events in life cause you to reevaluate your circumstances. All of a sudden there is a reason to get things done. *Like a big kick in the butt of apathy,* Clem smirked as he pondered the concept.

As the washer chugged away Clem lit up a cigarette. All of the minor accomplishments this morning were having their desired effect on Clem's attitude. His step was a little lighter. His dark mood from the night before had improved. He wanted to keep the roll going. This surge of electric energy sparked him with ideas. He puffed away there next to the washer. It felt both exhilarating and odd at the same time. Maybe the coffee had jolted him. Maybe the fire was just the thing to get him off his ass and start living again. He could start some new projects like painting the house. Fall is perfect season for painting. Get that water heater replaced. He puffed and felt new. He thought of Rainey and horses for a second. The washer clicked into the spin cycle. He knew he was just spinning his wheels. This just couldn't last. Back and forth he battled. There were the recesses in the back of his mind that held years of pessimism. It would take more than one good meal, caffeine, and clean clothes to combat all the shit he carried around. But he also felt there were plenty of cavities in his mind that also held hope. He'd just have to open them up, set them free and shut off the fatalistic ones. He wondered whether or not he was just comfortable with his pessimism, a familiar zone that seemed to work for him. Maybe it was time to come face to face with who he was, or who he had turned into. Could he even remember who he had once been? That was a stumper. "Who had I once been?" That was the question. He puffed slowly. Then a weird taste bubbled up in his throat. Acid from worried coffee. It was a reminder that he was not out of the woods yet.

*Stop thinking. Start doing.*

He stubbed the butt in the kitchen ashtray and had a glass of water. He remembered the colored clothes on the line from yesterday. They probably smelled like smoke. He frowned, then glanced at Goofy. 12:10 PM.

Clem stepped up to the receptionist's counter and announced "Clem Everett, reporting for duty." The office receptionist, Mary Lou Becker, looked up from her computer screen and said, "I'll be with ya in a second, hon." She finished entering a previous patient's insurance and appointment information, closed the current screen and got up from her chair. Clem knew Mary Lou from the Saddle Club. She and her husband were church-going folk, steadfast and as nice as could be. She walked over to Clem and handed him a clipboard. "We haven't seen you for quite a spell. You're gonna have to fill this patient history form out and sign the patient privacy page." Clem sat down and fumbled with the pen. He hated doctors and avoided them as best he could. Most of the questions he filled in but guessed and bullshitted on the rest. He signed his name on the patient privacy statement and laid the clipboard on the counter and returned to his seat. There was a large round glass table in front of him with an array of magazines laid out in a circular fan. He pulled one out just to ruin the symmetry. It was a *People* Magazine. He flipped through the pages and stopped on the crossword puzzle. There were big boxes and not that many clues, so he started trying to answer them. Pretty soon he was frustrated. He knew none of the celebrities referred to and less about their fame. It made him feel old and out of touch, so he flipped the rag back on the heap and folded his arms, which made him flinch with pain. His knee bobbed rapidly while he waited. Then he spotted the *Pueblo Chieftain* with its headline, "Rattlesnake Fire Alarms Rye Residents" It gave him a cramp in his side and both knees were now bouncing.

"Made the frontpage Clem." Mary Lou commented from behind the counter. "Yes-siree-bob, a hot time in the old town last night," he retorted while scanning the article.

There was silence.

He read on.

When he got to the part about sending the complete investigation to the district attorney to determine whether a crime had been committed, he was in a full panic sweat and his knees had stopped bouncing. The room was silent except for the thumping of his heart. He waited. He hated waiting rooms.

A young woman appeared in the doorway at the end of the counter and called Clem's name. Clem rose and walked toward her. As he entered the hallway, she was standing next to a weighing scale. "Them's cute pajamas," he kidded, looking at her uniform. The nurse asked Clem to step up on the device. He did so and she moved the weights to and fro until the bar leveled. One ninety-one. She jotted it down and then she led him into an examination room and directed him to the high bench with white sanitary paper on it. She automatically asked him how he was doing. Clem put up his arms, raised his eyebrows and grinned. She smiled. The nurse placed a funny gizmo on his index finger for pulse and temperature then took his blood pressure. As she wrote in the file, she mentioned his pulse was fast and blood pressure was high. "It's a good thing I'm here with you." He said. She smiled without showing her teeth, closed the file, put the gizmo away and told him he would have to remove his shirt. She turned to leave saying that the doctor would be right with him. Then she left the room, closed the door and put the file in a holder on the other side. He heard her footsteps fade. His hand habitually felt for the pack of cigarette in his front pocket. His fingers tapped and touched his breast pocket as a person reading Braille. He sat there with his feet dangling and waited.

Dr. Tanner Gibson entered. His crisp blue shirt and blue and red striped tie cut the perfect image of a confident and successful doctor. He greeted Clem warmly then checked the file in his hands. He gingerly asked if Clem had put the fire out by himself. Clem chuckled but had no reply. He was on edge. Dr. Gibson asked who administered his dressings and Clem said the paramedics did. The doctor surveyed Clem's upper arms, shoulders and torso. Then he told Clem he was going to remove the gauze and take a look. He unraveled it from each arm slowly. Only the last wrap, close to the wound, was difficult. It was stained light yellow and stuck to the blistered skin in places. The upper hands, wrists and most of the forearms were swollen and deep red. All the hair was gone. Large blisters had formed, and portions of the flesh were scorched. Patches of blood appear from where the gauze had stuck to the skin. Dr. Gibson stepped on a lever at the silver waste receptacle and tossed the wad of gauze in and let the lid down.

"I'm going to wash your hands and arm with some antiseptic warm soapy water. It's going to hurt. Then I'll apply antibacterial ointment and reapply gauze bandages. The burns are on the severe side and you should be very attentive to their care. You'll copy my procedure, changing the dressings every two days. We'll have you start a regiment of antibiotics for twenty-one days. If you should notice infection, meaning large quantities of a greenish discharge accompanied by a high fever, call the office and get into see me."

All the time Clem nodded looking rather pale. Dr. Gibson continued.

"What have you been taking for the pain?"

"A couple of 500 mg. Tylenol."

"Is it working?"

"Sorta."

"I'll add Demerol. Are you allergic to anything?"

"Doctors."

"Well that's fortunate," said the doctor, "because I'm actually a veterinarian."

"That's good, doc. I prefer vets."

"Remember to change the dressings every two days and start the antibiotics immediately. I want to see you in two weeks."

"I'll do that, thanks."

Dr. Gibson finished writing out the prescription and handed it to Clem. "Oh, and by the way stop playing with matches!" he threw in for good measure. He left the examination room.

Clem let out a sigh of relief. He struggled with his shirtsleeves and did his darndest to tuck in his shirttail by poking his fingers around the waistband inch by inch. He put on his hat and stopped at the receptionist's counter, made an appointment in two weeks and asked about his bill. Mary Lou said they'd bill him and not to worry. He left.

The pharmacy was located behind the medical center next to the Valley Market. Clem pulled out of the parking lot and immediately hung a hard 180-degree left turn into Valley Market's parking area. He parked in front of the pharmacy and pushed through the glass doors. He handed a young girl his prescription.

"Do you have an account with us?' she asked.

"Na, I'll just pay for it."

The girl took the prescription and went to a computer next to the cash register. She entered information and walked over to the pharmacist. They exchanged words and she came back.

"It'll be about twenty minutes."

"You're kidding."

"Everybody just got back from lunch and we're catching up."

"OK, I'll wait around."

Clem looked at the clock hanging above all the aisles of medicine. 2:30. This is gonna be close he thought and lip spit.

Clem walked through the throughway connecting the pharmacy with Valley Market. He saw Tessa Armijo at the checkout line. She called to him.

"Hey, Clem."

He lifted his chin in acknowledgement and approached.

"Hey, Tessa."

"Ain't you got better things to do than start fires?"

"It wasn't me, it was lightning."

"You and white lightning."

They both gave a chuckle.

"How you doing?" looking at his bandaged hands.

"Doc says I'll live, unfortunately."

"Damn the luck. I read nineteen acres burned."

"Just brush and trees and one old tractor."

He wanted to get the hell out of there. Tessa was the beehive of gossip in the valley. She had a way of embellishing the truth until it had a life of its own. New truth with a sting, but it was the truth according to Tessa.

Clem pointed at the cashier, "You gonna lose your spot."

Tessa moved up in line.

"Gotta go get a few things," he waved to her and went back in the pharmacy.

At the counter he asked the girl where gauze bandages and a bottle of antiseptic spray were. She pointed to aisle three and said, "First Aid."

Clem brought the items to the counter and asked if he could leave them there until his prescription was filled. Then he went to his truck for a cigarette. He lit up in the cab and it filled with smoke. He rolled down the window and did his dry lip spit. The days ahead weren't going to be easy. He'd have to do a lot of sidestepping or probably just keep his damn mouth shut. *It was an accident and accidents can happen to anyone,* he thought. He knew he was taking people's comments personally as if they all believed he'd started the fire on purpose or out of pure carelessness. *What did they know?* They knew Clem was a card. Their sympathies ran as deep as his jabs, hollow and superficial. Maybe because he was never serious, always sarcastic. For the first time, he felt that the tables had turned, and *they* were all giving *him* shit now, like he'd given them for so long. Maybe he was being paranoid. It shocked him to even consider what other people thought of him. He never did before. But he had never had such a major public fuckup either.

He flicked the butt out the window and went back in the pharmacy. At the counter the girl had seen him enter and had his prescription ready. She tallied the items, rang it up, punched a button on the register and tore the receipt off. He handed her a check and his driver's license. She stamped the

check and handed back his license and the receipt.
Clem put his fingers through the bag loops and left.

# Six

## Friday, 13th Afternoon

When Clem rounded the corner on Cuerno Verde road he saw two official vehicles parked in front of his house. He pulled his truck into the weeds next to the gate. He consciously snubbed his cigarette out in the cab's ashtray. Reaching over for the bag he took a deep breath and said to himself, "OK, let's get this over with." He bumped the door open with his elbow and slid out. At the same time both Sheriff Dayton and a uniformed man, who Clem didn't know, exited their vehicles. He met them at the front wire gate.

"Good afternoon Mr. Everett," said Sheriff Dayton. "This is Mr. Thorton Walker, with the U. S. Forest Service. He will be assisting me with the investigation."

Clem didn't offer his hand, neither did they.

"Why don't we head into the house? I want to put this bag down. My arms are killing me."

"That sounds like a good idea."

Clem kicked the gate open. The dogs ran out from the porch and jumped up and down in front of him.

"Don't worry. They won't bite."

The three men entered the house and the door closed behind them.

Clem invited the men to have a seat while he put the bag in the kitchen. He came back to the living room and sat in a chair facing the men on the couch. Sheriff Dayton inquired about Clem's hands. "Doc said I'll live." Clem didn't feel like finishing his joke. Dayton moved on.

"Mr. Everett, we're following up on the report submitted by Chief Hickman. He spoke with you yesterday evening. Is that right?"

"Yeah, I told him what I thought happen."

"According to your statement, you collided or ran into a boulder?"

"Yeah well I guess I wasn't paying attention. Just ran over the damn thing."

"And then what happened?"

"Well, it scared the bejesus out of me. I guess that boulder went right between the wheels and when it got to the swather it made a hell of a sound. It just about threw me out of my seat. You know, I didn't think much of it at first. It must have shot out a load of sparks."

"Let me get this correct. The blades hit the boulder."

"Yeah, made the tractor jerk and the swather shimmy and jump. I didn't stop right away 'cause there wasn't much I could do about it then. Everything was still working okay, so I figured I'd check it out later, straighten a blade or two or smooth out the dings. So, I just kept on cutting."

"Do you remember the approximate time of the incident?"

"You know, things pretty much just got wild after that. I ran back and tried to stomp it out. It wasn't too big then. Throwed dirt on it and patted it with my hat some. Then I was pounding it with my hands, but boy it just took off. I had to get away, it was real hot."

"That was probably a wise thing to do. In some cases, adrenaline makes people think they are indestructible. Then what occurred?"

"I hightailed it to the house and called 911."

"From this report, you told Chief Hickman the time was about two o'clock."

"That's what I thought."

"Your 911 call came in at 2:15 PM."

"Like I said it got crazy wild. I can't remember exactly what time it was you know."

"I understand."

"You know, now that I think of it, the operator said the fire had already been reported."

"That is correct." Dayton flipped a page. "The first call came in at 2:05."

"Mr. Everett, I notice by the pack of cigarettes in your front shirt pocket and the ashtray that you smoke," observed Walker

"Yeah I do."

143

"Did you happen to be smoking at the time of the incident?" he continued.

Clem didn't answer right away. "I seriously can't remember whether I was or not."

It was quiet for a moment while both Walker and Dayton made notes in their files.

"As you might have guessed Mr. Everett, battling wildfires can be costly. The state's budgets are established, and other contingencies are in place to deal with disasters and situation like this. And it is our job to determine whether accident, human error, negligence, or arson is involved. We collect all pertinent information, physical and written and then make an analysis and decide. The process may take a week or so," explained Mr. Walker.

"Sure, yeah, I understand," said Clem.

"We'd like to take a look at the initial area where the fire originated, if you wouldn't mind?" Dayton said.

"Help yourself. You don't need me, do ya?"

"Actually, it would be helpful if you joined us and walked through what happened," said Walker.

The three men stood near the boulder. They went over the course of events once more. Clem made small gestures with his arms and Dayton and Walker pointed and kick the black ground with their boots. They made notes. Then all three stood around the boulder. Walker bent down and touched the boulder moving his hand across the scratch marks then made notes. He then meandered around picking up objects from the ground and inspecting them.

*He's looking for cause*, thought Clem.

The three men then started walking in the direction of the barn where the tractor was parked. When they arrived both Dayton and Walker got down on their knees and began examining the blades and rim of the swather. They then circled it, pointing as they talked and making notes. Clem answered all their questions.

After the inspection the three men walked to the front porch. They climbed the steps and stood in the shade. The dogs ran up and joined them. Both Dayton and Walker patted the animals then handed Clem their business cards. They told him if he had any questions, he could contact them at these numbers. Clem nodded and the men tipped their hats. Dayton and Walker got in their vehicles and drove off. Clem stayed on the porch and watched them leave. So did the dogs.

Clem was exhausted. He was sick to his stomach. Waves of heat rose up and pressed against him. He stood there, a drooping, sweaty, mushy human. He looked at the hill. The black hill stared back at him. The one fire truck was still on guard. He felt like nothing and the cloudless sky bore down on him in his infinitesimal existence. The weight of worries solidified in his legs. He could not move. Yet he was about to tip over. He made his dry lip-spit sound, then he lifted one leg and then the other. He went into the house.

Inside the living room he stopped. He thought he had to do something but forgot what it was. He dragged himself down the hall and then remembered he had left the clothes in the washer. Opening the lid, he got a whiff of mildew. The clothes had been sitting too long. He'd hang them and let the sun dry them. They'd smell of grasses, pine, and wind. One by one he plucked them out dropping them in the wicker basket. He went out to the clothesline letting the screen door slap shut behind him.

The grasses crinkled under his boots. It seemed everyday was getting drier and drier. His hands hurt as he pinched the clothespins and hung the damp clothes. He looked at his clothes, wrinkled and tattered. *When,* he wondered, *was the last time I shopped for new clothes?* He was surrounded by things weathered and worn out. He hung onto the clothesline breathing shallow breaths. "One foot in front of the other is all I'm trying to do." He murmured. He slid the bag of clothespins along the wire and continued hanging. Something dropped from a pair of pants. Something shiny. It was his wristwatch. He reached down in the grass and picked it up. *My haste is becoming my waste,* he thought. The watch was still running. He did the hula, putting it in his hip pocket.

Clem finished and walked back to the house with the wicker basket hanging from two fingers. He let it drop next to the washer and walked to the kitchen table. From the pharmacy bag he removed the antibiotics and painkillers then read the labels. He did battle with the childproof caps, swore up and down, and finally shook them out. At the sink he filled a glass with water and drank the pills down.

He looked at Goofy, 5:13, then filched a cigarette and lit it.

The phone rang five times before Clem heard it. It rang five more times before he went to the hall. When he picked the receiver up all he heard was the dial tone. He was too late. Clem listened to the dial tone for a while then hung up. He went into the living room and sat on the couch. The sun shone on him from the west window. He sat there in the hot glow. To him, everything then felt like the dial tone. Even and steady. He closed his eyes laying his arms on his thighs. He felt his shoulders ease down. He sat there like a deflating tire waiting for the rims to bottom out. It felt good. He was so tired. He could see the glow between the slit of his eyelids. It twinkled and shimmered. The dial tone was fading. He drifted off to the lake of skimming stones . . . Ten stencil-like reflections of sun ricocheted off the water. Clem floated on the ripples the stone had made. He followed one further and further out. The ripple surrounded him and caressed him. He floated like a leaf. Like a fluff of cottonwood seed. He was so tired.

Clem opened his eyes slowly. The hot glow was on the other side of the room now. He had fallen asleep. The sun hadn't gone down behind Cuerno Verde yet. *A nice nap*, he thought, then picked some goo from his eye and stretched. He got up and went to the kitchen. Goofy said 7:30, and a shadow engulfed the room as the sun dropped behind the peak. Clem decided to gather the clothes from outside. At the back door Banjo and Sticker met him and followed. He rhythmically unpinched the pins and dropped the clothes in the basket. The mindless work felt good. He smelled the clothes one by one. *Pretty fresh*, he thought. They still had detergent scent. The brand of detergent that Rainey had always used . . . that he still used . . . maybe so he could still smell her. He knew he still loved her or kept a love for her in the box of his heart, like the secrets hidden away in the drawers, buried in the words of long-ago letters with faded addresses. He loved her still in the jumbled memories that he conjured. He knew that at one time the dots connected into a perfect line. A line that led him to know what love was. He knew that, even though it didn't last. That one spot in the box of his heart still burned, still ached, still loved. "A lonely old man having a love affair with a memory," he smiled. The last of the clothes were in the basket. His hands started hurting again. The painkillers were wearing off. The thought of a painkiller for lost love occurred to him. He returned to the house.

The phone was ringing as Clem entered. He put the basket down in the hall and answered it.

"Hello," he said.

"Clem."

The hairs stood up on the back of his neck. The voice so familiar and so strange.

"Gail?" he asked, knowing his sisters voice.

"Are you alright?"

"Wow!"

"I know."

"I mean, yeah. I mean everything's OK."

"National news aired a fire in Rye, Colorado and the more I listened the more it sounded like your place."

"I had no idea. I don't have a TV."

"Yeah, it was a big deal, evacuation of the town and stuff."

"It was a freak accident. Ya see, the blades of the swather sparked on a rock, caught the grass and it took off, but everything's okay."

"I called earlier but no one answered."

"Yeah it's been sort of a shitstorm around here."

"They said there were injuries?"

"Well, it was just me. My hands and arms got a little burnt, no big deal."

"Are you sure you're alright?"

"Yeah, I seen the doc and he got me on antibiotics. I should be fine."

"Is there anyone there with you?"

"I'll be fine." He nipped it.

"Okay, okay. I just wanted to call. I'm glad you're alright."

There was a pause.

"Listen," she said, "I know you're probably right in the middle of something, so I'll let you go."

Clem didn't know what to say, or *how* to say anything in that moment. "Yeah, well thanks for thinking of me."

"Okay. Take care. Oh, by the way, happy birthday."

"Okay, bye." He hung up. And before he realized it, she was gone. He should have said more. Should have asked how she was doing, anything.

He had her number and could call her right back, but the call had caught him so off guard. He started kicking himself three ways to hell about it and chewed the inside of his cheek. *What did I really have to say to her? I'm sorry? Yeah, that could have been a good start.* "Fuck it, at least I talked to her. That is what it is. Just accept it. She's the one who cut the ties," he persuaded himself.

With a huff he picked up the basket and climbed the stairs to the bedroom. He emptied the clothes on the bed and started folding. The way his hands were, it was more like groping. Socks, shirts, underwear . . . just get them in the drawers.

As he worked, he thought of Gail. It dawned on him that she'd said Happy Birthday. Was it possible? No wait. "My birthday, shit." He thought it through a moment. *Yesterday was the twelfth. Today was the thirteenth. Mom died on Friday the thirteenth. I married Rainey on the thirteenth of May.*

Thirteenths loomed large in Clem's life. He sat on the edge of the bed. *Today is the thirteenth, tomorrow is my birthday,* he mused in quiet thought. He was stunned that Gail had even mentioned his birthday. When he thought of her the first image that always came to mind was of the two of them sitting on their parents' backyard steps. He was probably three and she was four or five. It was summertime and they were eating watermelon. They'd both be covered in watermelon juice and spitting black seeds. Spitting the seeds seemed the most wonderful thing in the world. Laughing in the sweet joy of youth. Sitting there all sticky next to your best companion. Your best friend. The person you'd been through everything with. His sister. So safe. So easy. Clem knew these were the memories that made you forgive, made you look past the faults of family because you had shared the formation of their souls and characters, a freckle on your arm for the rest of your life.

He should have said more. He stripped the sheets off the bed and replaced them with clean ones. He wanted some order and control. His head was in a state of chaos, so he ordered his surroundings. Maybe, he pondered, if he cared about himself more, he would care more about other people. Sort of a rub-off thing. Or was it the other way around? If he cared about others more, he'd care more about himself. "Whatever . . . my hands hurt." He carried the basket downstairs to the laundry room. He was done being the domestic king for the day. It was time for antibiotics and painkillers.

In the kitchen, he made a peanut butter and jelly sandwich to go with the pills, then sat down. At the table he neatly placed the sandwich, medicine, and a glass of water in front of him. He had the odd ingrained impulse to cross himself for a prayer. A slew of memories flashed past him . . . the family saying grace before dinner, his sister and him giggling under their breaths, Mom and Dad casting dour looks at them. He knew it was Gail's phone call that was triggering all these bullets from the past. Goofy's second hand was bobbing on three then dropped to five. It was 8:20, he swallowed his pills and ate the sandwhich.

Clem chewed, silently. He was chewing on the future. How would the investigation pan out? How would he be able to cut winter wood with his hands? How would he face his neighbors and the town? Where the hell did that cigarette go when he hit the boulder? Clem chewed, connecting the dots. He still couldn't get over that it was his birthday. Sixty-six. He drank the water and lit a cigarette. The combination of pills and peanut butter wasn't good. He placed the glass in the sink and let the dogs in. Their water bowl was empty, so he filled it and went upstairs. Standing next to the nightstand he did the hula getting his wallet, keys, and wristwatch out of his trousers. From the nightstand he picked up Big Ben and wound it then took all his clothes off. The sheets were cool. His hands and arms burned. He tried to relax. Maybe if he thought of Rainey he could sleep.

He remembered one birthday trip with her to the Grand Canyon. He had been driving all morning and they had stopped for gas. The filling station was a typical tourist trap. Authentic white aluminum teepees set against a backdrop of magnificent red cliffs. It was her turn to drive. She got in behind the wheel cheerful and excited. He told her he was going to take a snooze back in the camper shell. So, he got out and walked to the back but needed to take a leak and went to find the restroom. When he came back out, she and the truck were gone. He frantically looked around and caught a glimpse of her turning onto the highway a half a mile away. He stood there in disbelief watching her merge into to traffic and then vanish. After he realized she wasn't coming back he started walking towards the highway. He hadn't a clue what to do. When would she notice he wasn't back there? He waited at the off ramp for an hour before she showed up. She pulled off the road and jumped out in tears. She ran up and flung her arms around him crying, "I'm so sorry." He could still feel how hard she had hugged him then. It turned into the best birthday present story ever and they'd tell it time and time again and laugh and laugh and laugh. Clem fell asleep in the candlelight of Rainey's laughter.

# Seven
## Saturday, 14th Morning

Clem hated the idea of hell. He only used the word when things went to shit. The place itself was a figment of some zealous priest's imagination. It was a place created to scare the shit out of ignorant people to get them to toe the line, the ultimate tool of control. But he did like the idea of heaven. For the past few days he had envisioned his ideal heaven. Time after time he looked out at the golden yellow upper field, unscorched by the fire. It had a vastness that invited you to walk within it. He had been swept away by its beauty from his first walk there. He liked that he could touch his heaven. He had laid in his heaven under the blue sky many times and thought how the blue sky was heaven's compliment. He thought about the little boy that had hanged himself. *Did the boy have a heaven that he could touch?* Clem enjoyed the idea that if he were to die, he could die in this yellow heaven right here under the watchful eye of Cuerno Verde, dissolve into the breath of the universe, his atoms mingling with the earth. *Whatever was responsible for everything probably wouldn't mind if I park my bones right here.* He'd give his thanks and eventually blend in with the scenery.

He never spoke of his heaven to anyone, not even Rainey with whom he had shared so many private thoughts. She was easy to share things with. It wasn't that you *had* to tell her, it was more like you wanted to. One day she asked how he came to be called Clem. It wasn't Rainey that was asking, it was her penetrating questioning eyes that evoked an answer. He told her that his mother wished to have another baby girl and had already picked out the name Clementine, after the little miniature oranges, or were they tangerines. But she'd had a boy instead and so she shortened it to Clement then even shorter to Clem. Rainey smiled and loved the story. Throughout his whole life Clem had been embarrassed to divulge the origins of his moniker. Rainey actually gave him a sense of pride to bear such a name. When he was with her, he never had to hide or defend who he was. In his eyes it made her all the more beautiful. He couldn't remember if she knew that or if he had ever told her or if they both had taken it for granted. What else had they both taken for granted?

Clem bit down with his eyelids as he lay in the cool sheets and savored his morning thoughts trying to get a jumpstart on a positive attitude. The night's sleep had been surprisingly sound. He lingered awhile more in the waking morning haze before his arms began to ache.

After breakfast and his prescribed dosage of meds he fed the dogs and went to the barn. At the corral Clem haltered the mare and led her out to the upper field. As he walked back to the barn, he looked at the old horse trailer pitched forward on its tongue. "Babysitting dead dreams," he mourned. He was holding on to the past tenuously with a rusting trailer and an aging horse, both he had done nothing with for years. He walked up to the trailer and kicked the flat tire. He wiggled the loose fender then dry-lip spit. *I could weld that together, give her a paint job and pack the bearings. She'd be good as new,* he mused. He lit a cigarette and kept staring at the trailer. He looked back at the mare, kicked the tire again and looked at his hands. He felt the consequences of his age. He felt all the work that each project would require. He looked at the house with its peeling paint and weathered siding. Where would the money come from? He had a pile of dots. He watched a brown gray grasshopper bang into the side of the trailer and bounce off into the tall stems. Was this the grand plan of life? Take off, bang into something and fall willy-nilly? He had done his share of banging into things then healed up, only to repeat the cycle over and over. If he'd learned anything over the years, it was that he was tired of that cycle. "I'm damn tired." He coughed and wiped the perspiration from his forehead.

It was hot standing next to the trailer, so Clem went into the corral and the shade of the barn. He felt nauseous and the inkling of a panic attack. He leaned against the inside of the barn taking deep breaths. His chest hurt and he coughed some more. "Too many cigarettes and fire smoke," he admonished himself. After several minutes, he settled down. It was too early in the day to get lost in feeling sorry for oneself. He picked up a shovel and started scooping up manure and pitching it onto the pile on the east side of the corral. The work was slow going because of his swollen hands. After, he filled the mare's water and forked a few flakes of hay into the feeder. Clem was facing the day in little increments.

As he left the corral, he saw a fire truck pulling into the gate at the lower pasture. *They must figure it's not completely out,* he thought. A crew member shut the gate and Clem waved to him. He waved back, got in his truck and drove to the base of the hill. Clem continued to the fence line and looked at all the black ground and charred trees. The lump in his throat was almost unswallowable as if something was trying to come up. He knew what it was . . . the anger, helplessness, guilt and fear. They were down there in need of release. He swallowed anyway and lip spit three times. It was funny how a grown man can feel just like an infant sometimes, wanting a hand to hold or a shoulder to cry on, someone to rock him to sleep with a goodnight song. Clem knew that old men still have infants trapped inside them. They still have adolescents and teenagers and young men imprisoned in that old-man mind. That is what it means to be a grown man.

On the far ridge a couple were making their way through burned pines. Clem recognized them to be the Galways. Hopefully they hadn't spotted him. He was not ready to face them yet. He turned and walked back to the house as if he hadn't seen them. His fire had destroyed their backhoe. Luckily that was all. Today was Saturday so he would wait until Monday to get in touch with his landlord, Earl Larkin and check if his insurance would cover the cost of the backhoe. Although he wasn't in any hurry to do so right now, considering he had been avoiding opening any of the letters Earl had sent.

Clem drank a glass of water at the kitchen sink. He glanced at Goofy, 9:24 AM. He felt the urge to get away. After all, today was Saturday, and it *was* his birthday. It was the perfect excuse to dodge any responsibility. TR's Country Store in Rye would be open. He would buy a paper and stock up on smokes. He'd try and act normal.

Birthdays were not something Clem celebrated anymore. In fact, for the past ten or so years he'd simply ignored them. At his age birthdays came too often. He thought that after forty birthdays should only be every ten years. That would be a significant amount of time to recognize and commemorate. Forget presents, everyone who came would have to prepare a story. It would be like a living wake. "Of course, one would have to have friends," Clem snorted. His friends had either died off, lived in other states or weren't his friends any longer. He had replaced nearly all of them with working, marriages and selfish personal pursuits over the years. In his self-imposed hermitage he'd lost touch with friends he still had and pretty much most of the world. *Just one less tradition,* he rationalized.

Clem started the truck and backed out of the weeds in front of the gate. He drove slowly looking at the lower field pretending like it wasn't his. He shook his head back and forth. "Damn! It still looks bad," he said. There were several cars pulled over to the side also looking at the black field and hillside. He sped up and fled.

TR's was located on Boulder Street next to the schoolbus compound in downtown Rye. In the twenties the building had been the high school gymnasium. Then in the nineties it had been converted to apartments and a convenience store. From the front entrance there was a view of the east side of Rattlesnake Hill a half a mile away. At TR's Clem parked and got out. He'd make his appearance short and sweet. He flicked his cigarette at the same time he pushed the truck door shut and went into the store. He grabbed a paper and stood at the counter. There was only one other customer in the store, Malerie Kotch. Malerie had lived in Rye her whole life. She drove a school bus as had her father before her. She and Clem were acquainted. She looked up and Clem gave her a nod.

"Holy smokes, Clem. Ain't you got better things to do than try and burn the town down?" she asked with a broad grin.

"Aw come on now, Malerie, I was having a heck of a time getting that barbeque started, 'til I threw the gas on it."

"Well that explains everything except what you were cooking." She looked at his hands and arms. "My, my, are you okay?"

"Yeah, just third-degree sunburn. Forgot my sunblock." They both chuckled and Clem had a coughing fit. He turned bright red.

"Dear Lord! You all right?"

"A lot of smoke the last day or so. I just need to have a cigarette."

"You know it was a madhouse down here when they cancelled school on account of that fire. They had us dropping kids off at the Methodist Church. You should have seen it, kids and parents running every-which-a-way. I'm surprised nobody got hurt." Her voice was rising in volume and timbre as she spoke.

There was a pause.

Clem looked down and didn't know what to say.

"Well," she continued, "you stay out of trouble, you hear and no more barbequing." She picked her bag up and made her way to the exit, then turned and called back, "Oh, by the way honey, Happy Birthday," gave a wave and trotted out.

Clem was stupefied. How did she know? He put a *Chieftain* on the counter and asked for a carton of Marlboros.

"Soft or hard," the teenage girl at the counter asked.

"Hard." He stared at the three nose rings, maroon streaked hair, spiked wristband and all black attire. He had never seen her before. She turned and bent over to reach the carton. As she did so, a tattoo of Felix the Cat was exposed on her lower back above the left hip.

"You get that in the marines?" he said working his best charm.

"Yeah." As blunt as can be, she rang the items up without looking at him.

Clem opened his wallet and said, "You better just make that two packs. I'm celebrating my birthday and I'm cutting back."

The girl spun around, put the carton back, and grabbed two single packs and rang up the purchase without a word.

Clem walked out to his truck, tossed the newspaper into the cab and lit a cigarette. He stood there thinking that the teenage girl probably thought he was a dirty old geezer. The funny part about it was he thought she was probably right. He quickly made a mental inventory of his appearance. Soot-scuffed boots. Manure-stained pants. A hat that looked like it'd gone through a fire. Two-day-old stubble. "Yep, a dirty old geezer!" He made the lip and tongue spitting sound and took a drag. His gaze ran across the tree line along Rattlesnake Hill. *Boy, from here you can't tell there was a fire at all*, he speculated. Clem smelled the air. The town smelled burnt. He wasn't keen on his high visibility there in the parking lot, so he got in the truck and began backing out. As he did so, Jacob Dresden, the kid from California cycled by. Clem pulled parallel to

Boulder and stopped. Jacob stopped, and held himself erect on the bike at Clem's car door window.

"I was just talking to your girlfriend in there." Clem nodded towards TR's, falling into his old patterns.

"What girl?"

"That young thing with all the nose rings."

"Oh, you mean Ajax?"

"My god, is that her name?"

Jacob changed the subject, "So did you pulla Bogart the other day?"

"A *what?*"

"You know, flick your cigarette." He mimicked the motion with a free hand.

Clem knew what he meant and was shocked at the kid's audacity. He kept up his tough proud façade of bitterness and rankling as he dragged on his cigarette, spit, and hissed between his teeth. "Swather sparked on a boulder. Just a freak thing."

"It was quite the show."

"You should have seen it from where I was." Clem didn't like where the conversation was going. "Listen sport I got the camera crew coming for a visit so I'll talk to ya later."

Jacob leaned off the truck and pedaled down Boulder toward Main Street. Clem flicked the cigarette butt into the street and stared at its smoldering form momentarily. Then with a second thought, he pulled the truck up near the butt, opened the door and stomped it out with the toe of his boot before pulling out onto Highway 165.

As he drove past the high school the last news van was retracting its satellite dish and packing up. "Bloodsuckers." He mumbled. He circled back, turning right at the Methodist Church. As he drove up Main Street, he saw several families unpacking belongings from automobiles and carrying boxes into their houses. He looked straight ahead and kept on driving. He was feeling bad all over again. It hadn't hit him until now how many people his fire had affected. He wondered if the only thing he would be remembered for was almost burning down the town of Rye. "Shit!" he said speeding up.

Clem noted that there were still some lookie-loos at the entrance to the lower field capturing the aftermath on their cell phone cameras. He pulled the truck into the weeds in front of the house. Before he got out, he lit a cigarette and watched them in his rearview mirror. It occurred to him to quickly go in before some inquisitive soul wandered up with a shitload of questions. Grabbing the paper, he slid out of the cab and beelined it to the porch. Banjo and Sticker met him. He went inside and locked the door.

In the kitchen Clem tossed everything on the table and plopped into the chair. The paper fell open to the front page. The headlines read "Rattlesnake Fire Lacked Venom." The fact that the fire chief had spun the angle that the fire would be beneficial to the forest did nothing to offset Clem's stress level. The fact that his fire made front page again for the second day in a row only added to his apprehension and sadness. With a finger he tipped his hat back and scratched his forehead and read on. Mention of "determination of whether anyone would be charged with a crime relating to the fire" had his adrenaline pumping. The surge made his armpits drip. He finished reading the article and stubbed his cigarette out. The idea of time was becoming increasingly puzzling to Clem. The more intensely negative an incident was the slower time went. The happier the incident, the more time flew. But in general, the older you got the faster time seemed to go. He reckoned his perception of time was at a snail's pace because of the fire and burns. "It's just taking forever," he whispered. He was searching for a safe place in his mind. A beautiful memory to latch on to. He chewed the inside of his lip and thought of licorice. The taste came to him instantly. He recalled picking at the dried flowers in his grandmother's garden, putting the seeds in his mouth and biting on them. The memory of the flavor filled his mind with end of summer adventures, neighborhood kids and kick-the-can, all floating there while the taste lasted.

Clem couldn't hang on to it, his hands hurt too much. He snatched a pack of cigarettes from the table and went out the back door. A dark weight pressed on him as he walked to the shed. It was hard to walk. He felt like he was walking uphill in a tunnel and the air was hot and thin. He wanted to talk to someone. If only he could talk to someone. He blew his breath out like a horse. Who could he talk to?

In the shed he stood in the shadows. The air stunk of gas and grease, machinery smells, engines and tools with his fingerprints and blood on them. He sighed in the comfort of familiarity. "I can talk to you," he said. He ran his swollen finger along the vise. "You are my oldest friends." Then he touched the anvil. "You are still here." He looked at the many toolboxes and large wrenches hanging above the workbench. "You have shaped my life." He put his hand on a box of old horseshoes. He began to cry. The tears dropped onto the dirt floor. They dropped there for a minute or two then slacked off. All the time there was just the silence of tears, but the shouting match inside Clem's head roared. He was performing a silent confession in his shed. His church, amongst the pews filled with oily implements at the altar of nuts and bolts... *I know I've squeaked by*, he thought. *I've done the minimum, surrounded myself with myself, created my own tradition of not giving a shit. I've gotten comfortable in my easy victories and sacrificed my future for my past. But I didn't always,* he admitted. *When I was young the world was smaller, wasn't impossible. I had a chance. But I don't know now, it's too big, it's too late, it's too much. I know what can happen. I can see what the end could be, and it scares me to death.*" These thoughts ended in an even quieter silence.

His absolution would be merely tears in the dirt. He knew the power of tears when there is no answer, solution or explanation. A good cry made everyone feel better. *At least I'm old enough to know that,* he thought, and that thought made him cry more. He was empty and lonely. He knew that too. He cried there a bit longer in the empty shadows and the lonely slits of light.

In the darkness Clem could see the dogs dashing past the shed and coming to the door. He pulled together what little was left of himself and let them in. From their body language he could tell someone was at the house. They stood silhouetted at the doorway of the barn looking out, barking, with ears perked.

As Clem left the shed, he spotted the tail end of his truck moving. For a second he thought he was hallucinating. But a second look confirmed indeed it was moving. With a get-up in step he rounded the house. There was a flatbed tow-truck dragging his truck onto the bed. Two men were there, one working the hydraulic winch and the other standing behind watching Clem's truck ease up the ramps.

"What the hell you doing?" Clem screamed and coughed.

The men just turned and looked at him.

"That's my truck. Who are you?"

The guy standing at the ramps said nothing but pulled an envelope from his pocket.

"God damn it! What's going on?" Clem said stomping up to the guy.

"Are you Mr. Everett?"

"Who wants to know?"

"I'm from Front Range Leasing and this is a repossession decree." He held up the official document for Clem to view then handed him his card.

"Yeah. I've been leasing that truck for the past two years," Clem said while looking at the guy's card.

"This document was issued due to non-payment for the past four months. We sent out a letter with a sixty-day grace period and then another informing you that if full payment was not received in the next sixty days the vehicle would be repossessed," the guy said calmly.

"I called your company and told them I was sending the payment," Clem desperately lied.

"We've no record of that." the guy said flatly. The winch stopped. The other guy started tightening a chain to the aisle with a come-along.

"God damn it! Now wait a minute here, let me call the company and get a check off. I need that truck," Clem pleaded.

"That's fine. Feel free to make the call, that's certainly up to you. But this vehicle is going back to the company." He put the decree back in the envelope and handed it to Clem. "Have a nice day," the guy said. By then the pickup truck was secured on the flatbed and both men got into the tow-truck and sped off in a cloud of dust.

Clem called out after them, "It's my birthday!" He stood there coughing with the card and envelope between his fingers. It had happened so quick that he was still reeling from shock.

The dots were dropping away one by one from bad connections. His faith was slipping. He'd become a romantic about life and nature ignoring the simple truth about the brutality of survival. He'd maintained the basic necessities. But this time it was different. This time it was in his face front and center. The things he had been recently ignoring were now coming back up to bite him. He was failing. His failures were curdling in his gut.

As his fears hemorrhaged, Sticker and Banjo started whimpering then howled. The sky cracked with a military jet fly-over. Clem stuck his fingers in his ears and trotted to the front door. It was locked. He kicked it and swore. He stomped on the porch in an Indian war-dance to the sounds of dog howls and jet turbines. He spewed out a litany of profanities at God and the military. All his rage fell on deaf ears. He stormed to the backdoor pursued by the dogs. At the screendoor he stopped. "I'm such an ignoramus. What was I thinking?" In anger, he slapped his straw hat against his thigh. It turned into a blind self-abusive fit. Instead of entering the house he walked determinedly to the upper yellow field. There he flung open the gate and kicked it. He didn't bother shutting it. Furiously he walked to the center of the field. He stood there fuming. The blood drum pounded in his head. Then he began to walk in a circle, then a wider circle. He was unwinding in ever widening circles. The anguish at his own stupidity made his mind and whole body feel numb. He felt like a big foot that had fallen asleep, flopping about, out of control, waiting for the blood to return.

As the pounding in his head lessened, he began to hear the sounds of his footsteps and the swishing of the dry straw. It was soothing. The circles were now very wide. His pace had slowed. The passing yellow straw was no longer a blur. He was watching his boots step one after the other. Finally, Clem looked up and his heart sunk at the sight of the blue, blue sky. "I have no blue sky in me." He walked on. This was the first time in his life he had ever felt so utterly vulnerable. He began experiencing a cascade of memories. Things that had happened for the first time. His first baseball caught. His first bike ride. His first cut. His first kiss. His first car. His first love. His first death. All these firsts fell on him as he walked. A lifetime of firsts falling like a waterfall of glitter on him. Tiny, glassy memories. *An awareness blossoms when a first happens*, he thought. Clem was deep in that awareness. His circle continued.

An hour had passed, and Clem was now standing near the Appaloosa. She looked at Clem, twitched her ear and flicked flies from her rump with her tail. It was quiet, a giant blue sky quiet. He stared at the mare and ran down some ideas. He'll call the bank on Monday and maybe arrange for a loan. He'll then call the leasing company and try and get the truck back. He'd have to do something even though it would be a long shot. He had nothing much to lose now.

Maybe, he mused, the universe was sending him a message that it was time to move on. Shed his material skin. Unload the accumulated dead weight of thirty years. Right now, it didn't sound that bad. He was tiring of responsibility, responsibility on any level. Is that what got people up in the morning? This could be his new goal, the goal to shed responsibility of any kind. He would get up every morning feeling free. What would that be like? This was new. Clem was getting nauseous and shaky. He was used to burdens. He'd lived with them his whole life like everyone else. What would it be like to be free of burdens? If things continued as they were, he'd know sooner or later. He entertained these ideas in the yellow field under the giant blue sky, the Appaloosa and he together in the quiet.

The last few days had been a time of apprehension and a subconscious fear of coming home to nothing. *Gone up in smoke, as they say.* The town had suffered that fear. Clem was starting to realize that fear. Losing everything because of a deep-seated desire to do so. Get out from under it. End the pointless struggle of keeping the ball rolling. It wouldn't be starting over; it would be starting new. His fear would be driving it, this *starting new.* What would that be like? He had been in *the old* for so long that it was comfortable and *the new* might be hard. He was used to his old comfortable burdens.

Clem's teeth began chattering in the broad daylight. The hot day brought a cold sweat on him at the same time. New fears were not fun, he surmised. He wanted to sleep on it. He sat down in the field next to the Appaloosa, in his vast yellow space. He wished he could go to sleep, period. He closed his eyes and the yellow space went dark.

In the realm of lost inconsolable space there are images that help magnify the imagination, where the surrealism of reality beckons to the courage of belief. On that edge the believer can go either way, believe or make-believe. Clem teetered there on the edge. Like the little boy, with the noose around his neck, teetering on the chair before it slipped out from under him, hanging in the short suspension of no return. The only mistake the boy made, in Clem's way of thinking, was doing it too early in life. Clem thought it more reasonable to do it late in life when the body was failing and there was nothing ahead but pain and expense. He had no lessons to share. He had no one, if you didn't count the mare or the dogs. No one would miss him.

Clem was in a space alone, alone with his worst thoughts. For every constructive idea he came up with, he'd find two destructive ideas to negate them.

Maybe it started with that Sunday ride when it began to change . . . they had an open invitation to ride on Chris Richards' property way up on Old San Isabel Road about five miles northeast of Clem's place. Chris' property was a hundred acres that ran above the south fork of the Muddy River. It was a lovely day and he and Rainey were chit-chatting about maybe riding down into the canyon along the river. While entering a small grove of pine and scrub oak, Clem's horse stumbled upon a hen turkey with her brood of chicks. The hen skirted out from under some scrub oak and fluttered a horrific sound with its feathered wings, which spooked the horses causing a chain reaction. Clem's mare reared but he hung on. Rainey's horse jerked to the side and bolted to the right. Rainey was thrown and her leg was temporarily lodged in the stirrup and then she went down hard. It took a moment for the commotion of horse and fowl to subside and when

Clem looked, Rainey was on the ground motionless. The slow motion of dread was heavy. Clem quickly caught her horse and secured both animals to a tree. Rainey was now trying to sit up when Clem ran to her. He was repeating, "Try not to move," and put a gentle hand on her shoulder. He slowly began questioning her about possible injuries and assessed the situation. She was dazed and had some abrasions to her face, eyelid and hand. There was a small laceration to her inner wrist, which was bleeding. She said she could not move her leg at all. After a while he was able to get her straightened out and examine the leg more thoroughly. It was a sight. Swelling had already begun and there were two long abrasions that ran crosswise to her calf muscle. She could not straighten her leg. Bruising started and they still had to somehow get back to the trailer. They both concluded there was no bone broken but there may be a torn tendon or ligament and some muscle damage and there would certainly be one hellacious bruise. After Rainey felt stable enough to rise, they had to search for one of her boots, which was torn from her other foot. Clem finally got her mounted and they slowly worked their way back. To Clem it seemed forever to get back to the ranch, unload the horses into the corral and drive to the emergency room.

After the examination the doctor determined there was no broken bone, but much muscle tissue damage and a serious concern for possible blood clotting. She was told to keep the leg elevated and to ice it. Visits to a rehabilitation therapist were recommended. He insisted she get and wear a compression sock and stay off it until the swelling reduced. It took several months before she could put all her weight on it and get around. Clem somehow felt responsible for the incident and internalized his failure for her safety. Rainey tried to console him, but he fixated on it. The pressure of recuperation and his trying to fix everything took its toll. Over time Clem's controlling issues and Rainey's independence and free spirit collided. Their relationship soured and ultimately deteriorated . . .

He looked up at the mare, "Come on now, get up," he urged himself. He stood and the mare nuzzled his side. He touched her mane and moved his hand down her back to the spots. He was trying to hold on to something. Catch hold of some thin thread of meaning. Something to stop this stampede of pernicious thoughts.

The spots began to move. Marbleize and converge. Rainey would have told a story about the origin of Appaloosa spots. Rainey would have filled the space Clem could never fill. The shades of brown. The shades of gray. All the shapes that love would fill. Ovals and oblongs. It was Clem's loss. He'd known it. "It's probably what chaps my ass," he said to the horse. His hand gently smoothed the hair over the spots then rested. "Tell me a story Rainey. Tell me so that I can listen to you talk. I like the sound of it." Clem felt the world get slower for a second. To him right then was truth. He did love someone. Her, Rainey, a letter in a box in the back of the drawer, more unconnected dots he'd forever ignored. Her, her raised eyebrow, the little twist in her cheek, her freckled nose. He was trying to let her fill the space again. "Please don't stop talking." The closer he got to his love of her, the more the spots moved. "Why don't they stop!" Clem worked it over in his mind. Was he in love with the idea of loving her? Was his love for her a sham? Did he really love her? Was his world spinning out of control because he could never love her? Never love anyone? Was he capable of loving anyone? Had he just assumed he could love?

The spots slowed. Love was not a pair of pants you put on and take off. The spots slowed more. Love was not one thing. The spots began to stop. Love is constant and never temporary. Clem saw why she had left. Now he saw that he hadn't respected love. Hadn't fully understood it. Tried to control love. Hadn't believed in its power. All these years of hiding his secret tore at his will. He had never fully faced his failure. He had seen a glimpse and it was terrifying. So, in the drawer it stayed. All the spots stopped. Clem was in the drawer. The secrets and letters flew at him like bees and bats. He flailed away with his arms to no avail. It was his price to pay for playing with and wasting love.

Clem smoothed the mare's hair again, shaking his head back and forth slowly. The chattering came back. The same chattering he had when he was growing up. A scared chatter. A cold fear. His space was knotty and tangled. He swallowed and tightened his jaw shut. With his other hand he reached for the bridle. The mare came along as he led her to the gate.

# Eight
## Saturday, 14th Evening

The light of day was in decline and evening with its dark eyes came searching. Clem sat on the divan and for a moment half of him was illuminated by the setting sun and the other half darkened by the gloom of shadow. He'd been sitting there for a long time mulling over the horde of dots and spots. There was no need for those spots and dots anymore, he reasoned. They had outlived their purpose. He could let go of that tradition. He stood up with effort and the oak floorboards creaked. His boots took him upstairs to the dresser. He labored opening the bottom drawer, huffing and grunting. From the drawer he lifted a small cardboard box and a tied bundle. As he steadied himself, he shoved the drawer shut with a boot. The things felt heavy to him, so he laid them on the bed for a moment. The room swelled and shrank. He picked the things back up and went downstairs.

On the table in front of the fireplace he laid the things down. In the dark room Clem pinched a pack of matches from his pocket. He then squatted between the table and fireplace. Holding onto the table he managed to sit down on the rug. He parted the fireplace screens and found a poker. From the table he pulled the bundle onto his lap and untied it. With swollen fingers he fumbled lighting the match. The flame brought the room alive. He picked the top letter off the bundle and lit its corner. A corona of blue and orange glowed. Then he gently placed it on the grate. The thing burned and curled. The stamp fluttered and lightly hissed with twinkling colors. The address went black.

Clem fed one after the other to the flames. He watched them burn with a curious patience, methodical in his numbness. It was time to let go. Who was he saving them for? He had no one to grow old with. He would be trapped in his maze of memories without a soul to share them. He could not relive them. It was time . . . and time, as he knew, was shifting more and more.

After a while the bundle was gone and only the ribbon that had tied it remained. He picked it up and smelled it. It was still saturated with a scent that was all Rainey. Every word. Every place. Every gift of thought. Every "love you", every "good-bye." Clem swung one end of the ribbon into the flame. The tip smoldered then caught. He held onto the other end, watching it burn. It radiated in colors of the past. He smelled Rainey burning, the scent of no return, and finally flung his end into the curling flakes of ash.

Burning the box and the rest of the secrets was easier. Clem viewed bits of envelope and cinder float and ascend up the chimney. He thought of how he and Gail would light their wish lists to Santa Claus on Christmas Eve. If they did not burn all the way before they disappeared up the chimney, your wish would come true. Innocence was bliss. Ignorance was bliss. The glowing undulating pile of ash was now bliss. Clem sat there until all the memories cooled. He lifted the poker and stirred the embers. They were so fragile, so delicate. They crumbled at the slightest touch. He had not made any wishes. He had not asked for anything as the mementos vanished into the dark ether. They were all the proof that had held him together, evidence, secrets, sweetness, sinew and guts that had made his failures tolerable.

Clem stood the poker next to the fireplace. The room hushed with the sound of freed secrets, that sensation of suspension before the swing falls back and you feel your own gravity. He was witnessing hundreds of vanishing points and endless horizons, then the room's silence. Just himself.

The light from a passing car dodged and dashed through the room like a terrified kid then was gone. Clem listened to the tires crushing the gravel on the road and fade. He managed to get to his feet and walk to the divan. He eased himself down and sat. Leaning back, he stretched out groaning as his legs came up. It was good to lay there. Good to let go of so many things. Things that had been heavy for so long. "That was a nice little birthday party," he muttered.

In the many-shadowed room Clem's eyelids were heavy. He let them fall. This rest turned into sleep, the kind that sneaks up on you when you think you're still awake. The many shadows fell with his eyelids. He slept.

The moon had arced into the night sky and now shone on Clem. It lit his tired skin and raked soft through his stubble. It was a fat moon and bulged out its fantastic rays. He woke and opened his eyes. They gleamed in the rays. He shifted and turned in the lunar blanket. "Turn out the light," he said half asleep. He half-slept and half-woke for the rest of the night. The night filled with half-dreams, half-fulfilled.

# Nine
## Sunday, 15<sup>th</sup> Morning

*The ringing was distant, like the ringing in your ears after a firecracker exploded too closely. Clem was running in the field and the ringing came again. He stopped running and opened his eyes . . .*

Clem sat up slowly. His body was stiff from the hard divan. The ringing continued. The room was already hot. He squinted in the radiant morning light. He bent toward the hallway, toward the insistent phone and rose from the divan. He picked up the receiver and paused before saying hello.

"Clem, is that you?"

"Yeah, who's this?"

"Earl Larkin, Clem. I hope I didn't getcha up."

"No, no, what time is it anyway?"

"Nine-thirty or thereabouts. I thought I'd catch you before it got too late."

"Just about to pour a cup of coffee," Clem fibbed. The pit of his belly started to somersault. He immediately sensed the reason for the call.

"I read about the fire and wanted to find out if everything was all right."

"Yeah, Earl. The lower south field burned and some trees up Rattlesnake Hill were lost but there was no damage to the house or any outbuildings. It just don't look too pretty."

"How are you faring? I read that you were injured."

"I managed to burn the heck out of my arms is all."

"I was concerned and a little worried, but I figured you were tied up, so I waited to call ya."

"Well I appreciate that, Earl. Yeah it's been pretty nutty here for the past day or so." He fell into the pretences of his jolly old self.

"Listen, Clem, I know this is a bad time, but did you get my letters?"

Clem had his fingers on the pile of mail next to the phone. He chewed the inside of his cheek and tapped the pile. "As a matter of fact, Earl, I was looking for your letters just the other day. I been working on the inside of the house, painting and fixing windows. Somewhere in this mess I misplace those letters. I been meaning to give ya a call . . ."

"Clem," Earl cut in, "you remember I sent those letters after we settled on the last late rent payment."

"That's right I remember, but I'm still trying to get my finances sorted out. It's taking a little longer than expected, that's all."

"I've had your checks bounce so many dang times that I stopped cashing 'em."

"And I been bouncing from one odd job to the next."

"Well Clem, you could have called."

"I was, but . . ."

"Well, I'm gonna have to move on this. Some changes have come up in my life. I'm giving you verbal notice and will send a written notice that you'll receive in a few days. I am sorry but you have not responded or even contacted me for months now and I have no option."

"Now Earl, you're gonna have to be a little more patient about this . . ."

"Clem if you had read the letters you would have learned that my daughter is married now and is going to have a child. She and her husband have been temporarily living here with me and my wife. Her husband has been hired by a good firm in Pueblo and they will be moving into the house.

"Earl . . . you're right, I should have . . ."

"I tried to give you the heads-up of this new predicament. I explained, *in detail*, times, dates and reasons for this action and allowed leeway for you to make proper arrangements and time for your transition. Still I heard nothing back from you.

"I. Am. Sorry," said Clem stressing each word.

"I'm sorry too, Clem. I know you've lived there quite a spell."

"Earl . . . this is a bad time."

"Look, I'm not trying to be a hard-nosed son-of-a-gun, but the reality is they will be moving in. Please Clem, review the letters I sent you.

"Earl, I'm gonna need more time. I'm not doing all that great.

"I am sorry, you take care of those burns now." The phone went dead.

"Earl, Earl? Damn it, EARL!"

He hung the phone up and walked back to the divan to see if he was still asleep.

Had it all been a dream?

It had to be.

He sat down. Dust moved in the sunrays through the room. He laughed, then cried and then chuckled to himself, "When the shit hits the fan!" He laughed so hard he had a coughing fit. Falling back on the divan he laughed and coughed and wiped the tears with his dirty bandages.

"So, this is what it's like to hit bottom!"

After he calmed down Clem patted his shirt pocket for a cigarette. The pack was crushed from sleeping on it, but the cigarettes were not broken. He lit one and blew smoke into the sunrays. It swirled and dissipated. He made his little dry tongue and lip spit sound and lay there. The cigarette smoke eddied in and out of the rays where his runaway thoughts found temporary solace. He sang softly, "Happy birthday to you. Happy birthday to you . . ." For a moment he was about to ask for God's help out of some knee-jerk reaction but abandoned the notion as quick as it came. Why was it that the last straw was given to God? Why was it that we asked God to help clean all the shit up from the fan after the fact? Why wasn't man responsible for all of it? Maybe man was simply and inherently weak. Not physically weak, but not able to cope with the bombardments of contemporary societal demands. Some men's minds just could not process and deal with it constantly. They simply retreated or snapped. Clem had already retreated and now felt the snapping point was close. Where failure and regret double-teamed him, and farewell dust gathered on his boots. He was nearer to it than ever. He contemplated the crooked, bent cigarette between his fingers and said, "Well old buddy, you're starting to look like me."

Clem licked his finger and pantomimed three strokes in the smoke, saying. "Mentally, emotionally and *financially* bankrupt!" He was using Rainey's words, but it didn't matter it was his life and the words fit to a tee.

"Let's see now. I started a major fire for which I may be prosecuted. My truck was repossessed. I'm getting evicted. I don't have enough money for rent or to get the truck back. My arms are burnt, and I feel like shit and on top of that I'm talking to myself. Yep, that's about the size of it," he tallied. His whole life he had spoken to himself. He'd have endless internal conversation in his head, but now they were out loud. *When had that started and what did it mean?* It irked him to discover this new behavior.

"It's just my due and I'm reaping what I sowed," he said. "It's just like the fire. Sooner or later it had to happen. The time was right." He could go on and on and justify his whole life and whine over and over, *why me, why me,* but he knew it was pointless. It was his turn to be the sacrificial lamb in the cycle of fate. It was somewhat comforting to think that *fate* was a player in this calamity. Clem knew that fate was not random but rather like a row of dominoes. Each domino was a particular decision you made in your life and these dominoes are placed one after the other. After years of decisions something bumps into the first one and that's it, the row tumbles. The best you can hope for is a break in the cascading effect or a sturdy standing domino that holds up. Clem wondered what would stop the tumbling down of his dominos.

In the kitchen Clem heated water for coffee. His arms pained him dreadfully this morning. His immediate agenda was another cigarette, painkillers and coffee . . . in that order. His clothes were wrinkled, and he could smell himself. The bandages were stained from the oozing wounds. The smoke filled the kitchen and he kneaded his forehead. He did not look at Goofy.

After a while the painkillers kicked in. Clem grabbed the mug, stood up and went to the backdoor. It was still open. At the screen Banjo and Sticker were shimmying and looking up at him. "I left you little shits out all night, didn't I?" They cocked their heads waiting. He pushed the screendoor open for them then went back to the kitchen. He dumped kibble in both their bowls, spilling much of it, and then filled their water, spilling that as well. He left them to eat and walked to the hall.

As Clem passed the phone, he scooped up the pile of mail from the table and continued to the living room. He sat on the edge of the table in front of the fireplace. He began his second cleansing session by lighting the corner of a Truck lease late notice. It burned blue and he tossed it on the grate amongst the ashes. He systematically lit each notice and watched them be enveloped by the flames. Next were the letters from Earl Larkin.

As the flames rose, he picked the poker up, stirred the pile and added the rest of the junk mail. He held the poker in the flames, looking. He wondered about what he was doing. He thought about how misfortune and bad luck cause people to do rash things. He lifted the poker and looked at the glowing end. He remembered Rainey's best friend Chamisa. A mixed-up gal from Farwell, Texas. She had a scar on her arm in the shape of a heart with a cross on top. He had asked her about it one day. She told him she had branded herself with a coat hanger as a reminder of an awful divorce she'd gone through. He asked why she would want to remember that, and she replied, "So's I don't repeat the same mistake twice."

Clem turned the poker and said, "Too late for branding," and stuck it back into the flames.

There it was again. He puzzled over man's eternal reference to time. Why was it *too late*? Too late for what? Does time heal all wounds? How do the other creatures exist not having time, but only the continuous revolutions of dark and light, cold and hot, wind and calm, wet and dry, slow and fast, painlessness or pain? Was the idea of time one of the sparks of consciousness or the beginning of the most hellacious ass-chapper ever?

He smirked and lit a cigarette with the hot end of the poker.

Was there time inside dreams? He knew that time could go backwards in dreams. The little boy who hanged himself had stopped time. Do you ever save time or is it an exchange of time? Does time fly when you have fun? Clem knew in himself that the best time is when you've lost it completely like right before the fire, when he was captive in every detail of his surrounding world, when he was engulfed by his most loving thoughts. He stopped time, or stopped the *awareness* of it. It was a rich sensation to escape the tenuous grip of time. "That's the place to be." He made the dry, lip-spit sound, and repeated, "That's the place be."

The room had become stifling with the fire's smoke and consuming heat of the day. Clem stubbed his butt out on the fireplace bricks and went to the kitchen for a drink of water. The dogs were lying on the cool linoleum floor and hardly moved when he came in. As he drank over the sink he gazed out at the blackened hillside. All the fire equipment and trucks were gone now. The heavily treed crest on the hill had all burned away. All that was left of the once splendid rich knoll was a naked old man, stripped for all to see. He was embarrassed for the hill. He bent his head and choked off a sob, but his eyes moistened and finally teared.

Had he committed a Bogart and sinned against the thing he loved? The field.

A pounding erupted in his chest. He could feel it in his forehead. He thought his nose was running. Little drops of red splattered on the Formica countertop. Clem leaned over the sink and spit a bloody gob of sputum. His nose stopped bleeding. He rinsed his mouth out spitting again into the sink, this time not so much blood. With his eyes shut he tried desperately to conjure up an image of the moment right before the tractor and swather hit the boulder. Did he have a cigarette in his hand? As he leaned on the rim of the sink, he kicked the lower cupboard, startling the dogs. Again, the blackened field glowered at him from the window. "It's gonna take years to heal this wound," he said. "Maybe time will forget it." He certainly wanted to. It wasn't likely he would repeat the same mistake twice, at least not in this lifetime.

# Ten
## Sunday, 15ᵗʰ Later

The painkillers were on the counter. Clem took two more then found his hat on the kitchen chair. At the back screen door he clicked his tongue for the dogs. They came running. All entered the bright hot day. The dogs scattered and Clem made for the work shed. He pushed the old battered door open and walked into the shadows. After a moment his eyes adjusted. He was a bit vague on why he was there, but the work shed made him feel useful. It contained his tools. To feel useful gave him purpose. There was courage in purpose, and one could think once more of the future. The excitement of the challenge danced in his head until the let-down that *nothing would come of it* occured to him, and the exuberance faded. He wanted to feel useful and to have purpose. He felt adrift in this sea of bad luck. He so needed courage to stand up to these ill winds.

Clem was glued to an untenable situation. He was caught in an encroaching emotional rigor mortis from his inability to act on any major decision to change his life . . . he felt like a man seized in place. He had the mechanical apptitude to understand the *frozen bolt* and the pressure it would take to make it give. How could he apply that knowledge now, to his life? He would need the proper tool. He didn't feel he had it. *What was the proper tool? Pliers of Strength? Hammer of Belief? Chisel of Choice? Saw of Knowledge? Wrench of Friends?* He was out of his element. The whole situation had rusted tight into place. He tried to figure a way to budge it. He needed to forge a new tool to take on the frozen bolt of his life. The little boy who'd hanged himself did not have the right tools to undo his predicament. The battle of existence could not be won without the right weapon. He looked around the dark space, at the tools that had once given him purpose. Even the chainsaw that he might sell lent him a small spark of hope. But the pittance he would receive would not help much now. He would have to sell *everything*. People need time to prepare to part with their belongings. There are proper goodbyes to deal with. *That's if you care*, he thought. A bitterness had welled up in the last few days. A bitterness that left caring in the dry dust. It occurred to him that he'd stopped caring months ago. *Maybe,* he thought, *that's why my small world is collapsing.* The struggle to solve his dilemma persisted like an obsolete tradition that he so despised. He had outlived his usefulness. *I am useless*, he thought.

Clem was not thinking straight. He tilted his hat back and held onto the anvil on the workbench while his head spun with dizziness. His mouth was dry, and he felt he was going to vomit. The sickness passed as he stood there inhaling and exhaling with concentrated effort. Then he spun off the bench and went outside to urinate. He wavered and peed in the hot sun.

Afternoon did not arrive; it had been there all morning. Unusually hot. At seven thousand feet above sea level the sun sears your skin like bacon. You heed the heat and take shade often. Clem removed his hat and wiped his forehead with the stained bandages. Squinting in the hateful sun he saw the mare by the corral gate. He went there and haltered her and led her to the yellow field. On the way he picked two green apples from the tree. He fed the larger one to the Appaloosa and nibbled on the smaller himself. They were sour-sweet. The mare nudged Clem's backside for more.

At the upper gate he removed the halter, gave her the last of his apple then smacked her rear sending her off in a gallop through the tall straw.

She whinnied and flicked her tail as she ran. She would find a shady spot and lie in the dry grass, maybe give herself a dust-bath. *She would like that,* he thought. He watched her in the yellow field against the blue clear sky. The view nearly took his breath away. He wavered and had to grab the gatepost to steady himself. He left the halter hanging on the post.

For the next hour Clem chain-smoked, wandering from shed to corral to field then back to the house. He did not have a plan. He was hiding. Hiding from anything else the world would throw at him. He would busy himself with so much of nothing that it became a plan. False as it may be, it gave him time. It was Clem's clumsy way of sorting out his decisions. Procrastination in a symphony of movement. He hoped it would work. He hoped it would lead him somewhere. He hoped he could fool himself long enough so that he could not care.

As he came in the backdoor, he heard something. He went to the kitchen sink for water and painkillers. Then he heard it again. It was a knocking at the front door.

This would be the perfect time to ignore it.

It came again, a soft tentative knock.

He stopped believing in his fear and went to the door. He had not unlocked it yet this morning and fumbled in his attempt to open it. He was flustered by the time he swung it open. There on the porch stood Janet Galway. His neighbor. The intense sun made her small and doll like.

"Hi Clem."

"Janet," he stepped out on to the porch.

"I saw you working around the yard and thought I'd catch you."

"Yeah, just keeping out of trouble."

"Yes, we've had our share," she looked at him. "I've been meaning to stop by but it's one darn thing after the other. You know?"

"I know. I just hoped you weren't another stranger at my door."

There was that moment where both parties hold, for a split second, the flood of all the things they could say but feel helpless to do so.

"I'm so *damned* sorry about the fire and all. I still can't believe it." He shook his head.

"We're all very lucky. But, look at your arms. Oh, my Lord. Are you going to be alright?"

"Yeah, ain't that something." He lifted his arms for a better look. "I got blisters everywhere." His false laughter was painful.

Janet looked deep into Clem and took a step towards him with her arms outstretched. In mutual knowledge they gave each other a hug. Clem gently sobbed.

After a moment they released and she said. "You know we were worried about you."

"You're the bee's knees, Janet."

"Is there anything I can do." She smiled.

"You know what?"

"What?"

"I think I need another hug."

They hugged and laughed. Then laughed a bit longer. For an instant, everything was perfect.

"Well . . . okay, if you do need anything just give Jason or me a holler,"

"Thanks, Janet. I'll do that."

"No, I *mean* that," she pushed and met Clems eyes again with a penetrating look, then turned and left.

Clem watched her picking her way daintily through the overgrown weeds and stones to the road. She turned once to look back. Clem was still there watching her. She gaily waved and continued. Clem lifted his chin in return. He watched her recede into the heat, becoming smaller and more doll-like with each step. He thought of her walking all the way up the hill to check on him. Her concern. It touched him. He could still feel her hug, sense her presence. He shook his head as she rounded the bend and disappeared before her long shadow did. She had brought some magic with her. She had made him laugh. He had not laughed from inside for a long while. *Maybe there is hope*, he thought.

A Ford F150 rumbled down Cuerno Verde Road. Plumes of dust rose from the tailgate. The horn blasted and an arm came out the window. It was Malerie Kotch coming from her father's house. She waved and roared by. Clem lifted his arm halfway. It was time to retreat to the safe confines of his house. He was exhausted and nauseous.

Back in the house he was once more confronted with the reality of his unreal life. The slight refuge that Janet Galway had offered was little consolation in relation to the war he was waging. The room spun. Clem bit down with his eyelids to ward off the spinning and the flashes of things that began to appear in his mind.

From the hall he climbed the stairs to his bedroom. He entered the stale heat that had collected there. At the same time the room seemed cold and neutral. He felt nothing for the room. It had lost its comfort. He guessed why. He had cut the cord with his past by burning all the letters.

There were no more secrets to protect. The room had lost its air of belonging. There was no connection with that old existence. He existed now in a limbo that he had created by severing that tie to all that was precious. It did not matter now. Clem reasoned it was simply a tradeoff. A prison for freedom. He did not care about the room any longer. He was done with the negligence of time spent there. But he had to lie down.

Clem lay on the bed in a heap of numbness. The painkillers were doing their job. He could not feel the blisters that had popped. Or the wet ooze that seeped and smelt. He could feel the throbbing but it was painless. Images flashed when he closed his eyes. Images of the fire. Images of Rainey. Images of horses and places in his youth. Images of the field from above as he soared over it like a hungry hawk. He opened his eyes to stop the kaleidoscope. But he was tired. His eyes fell shut and again the onslaught of images harangued him. He held onto consciousness, keeping his eyes shut. The images swirled faster. The letters flew by. People's faces flew by. Clem, in many forms, flew by. Buzzards and bears flew by. He was falling into the yellow field. Then a wind began, and Clem passed out.

The sun had melted away over the earth's horizon and dragged the planet Mercury along with it. The rotation had let the dark pool of night fill the sky. The curved slit of moon hung from this black curtain. The stars were there too. The room looked over the field, and the view of it was yellow; even at night and the sound of the life in it got louder. The mice, bats, crickets, owls and spirits sang in an ancient din, carried to Clem's room on a warm breeze.

Clem lay there a bit longer and dreamed on the bed to Natures lilting serenade. Dreamed of the black, burnt field and the earth moving under it. Things that were not burnt. Things that only bloom after a field burns. Dreamed of Death . . . *Which is, afterall, only renewal and nourishment*, he thought. He dreamed of fall, and the leaves hurrying to the ground. Ferris wheels and sparklers. The promise of each spring spawning life. In this dream he was young with smooth beautiful skin and slender fingers. He was skipping stones and counting. The counting became a rhythmic sound as if someone or something was calling. He was standing on the lakeshore, and the lake became the yellow field. And as he stood there, he started to change. He grew older. He both *watched* the person growing old and *was* the aging person. He dreamed the call came from the yellow field. The call came into focus. As he aged, he watched himself dissolve into the yellow field . . . and then he woke up.

His eyes opened. He was on the bed.

He heard a dog bark. He waited. Heard the bark again and continued to lay there. He was unable to move. His mind had woken before his body, which was still in the dream. It was still locked there mingling into the field grasses and soil.

The bark came again.

Clem shut his eyes to go back to the Yellow Field. He was not there any longer. This time he woke with his body. Clem listened to the bark for some time before he sat up. He was in a dream hangover with the horrible feeling that some dreams can leave on you, some film of unperceived regret or grim futurity.

He sat on the edge of the hollow bed dangling his boots just above the floor. The dim room was black and white and out of focus. The barking continued. The bed was moist where he had laid, and he was so hot. He suspected fever but couldn't tell because it was so hot in the room anyway. He unbuttoned his shirt and inched it around the bandages. Then he stood up on weak legs getting his balance.

First, he went to the window. The bark came again. Banjo and Sticker were out there alternating barks at some invisible thing. Clem did not feel right. He felt his legs were going to fail him, so he returned to the bed and sat. Several barks passed, then he made his way to the stairs. He descended slowly, one stair at a time, holding fast to the handrail. His feet stepped down and forward, but with each step his hands were reluctant to let go of the rail, as if they knew their fate. At the bottom of the staircase he was breathing heavily and disoriented. He collapsed on the last stair, slumped over. His nose was running and in the faint light he watched dark drops land on his stale white bandages.

Laying there on the last step he floated in and out of consciousness. After a long span it was better, his nose had stopped bleeding. The blood had crusted over and hardened. His consciousness brought with it chills and now he was cold. The old Navaho rug was within reach. He pulled it around his shoulders like a blanket, and shivered. As he sat there he could not remember what he was doing or why he was there. He heard the bark again. *That was it*, he thought, *it was calling him.*

He pushed up and stood. Passing the hall table his boot kicked it and something fell to the floor. He heard it and kept on. At the back screen door, he rested. A breeze ran over him, and he pulled the Navaho rug closer around him. The call came again.

"Keep your pants on, I'm coming," he mumbled darkly. His boot kicked the door open and he leaned into the clean black night.

The call from the black summoned him again.

Clem was impelled to go towards the upper field. He traversed the ground in stabs and missteps, walking crookedly and staggering like a dog sniffing scents in three different directions. His fingers worked the gate open and he followed his boots through the yellow field. The dry grasses crackled like applause as his boots carried him along.

Clem felt the blackness of the night. The cold dark rays touching him. He felt the blackness of the lower field smearing black ashes on his skin. He felt the blackness in his life was connected somehow. His troubles and discontents were in some way merging. His careless actions and mental attitude were the cause and effect of the calamity that permeated his existence. He tried to make the little habitual tongue to lip spitting sound but could not feel his lips or tongue. He zigzagged on, into the field.

When he was out of breath he stopped. He sensed that Banjo and Sticker were now with him wiggling and panting. Clem flopped down into the raucous pillow of the grass. The dogs licked his face laughingly. He felt welcomed by the chorus of the night and the enormity of the field.

Clem raised his eyes and looked at the yellow carpet of straw that unfolded in front of him, the house and corral in silhouette against the burnt knoll. The lower field did not look as desolate in the starlight. It almost looked as it once did before all this. That made Clem warmer under the woven blanket. He looked at the canopy of stars above him. They seemed to dance and twinkle with blues and reds so vibrantly that Clem's jaw fell open. The Big Dipper looked like it was overflowing. The Small Dipper with Polaris in the north glowed and pulsated. Clem found the constellation Cassiopeia in her matriarchal glory and imagined her looking down at him lovingly.

All this Clem took in sitting there in the yellow field. He tried to remember the last time he'd come out to look at the stars, but he could not remember. He had no memory, only the now. Only now, under Cuerno Verde's monumental peak. Now, in the presence of towering pines, Douglas fir and Blue Spruce. Now, beneath universes and galaxies, he began to feel no longer alone.

The dogs squirmed, making gentle restless noises and perked their ears. Clem heard the crackling of dry grass and soft clomps of the Appaloosa approaching him. The mare halted a foot from Clem. She snorted and her warm breath filtered over his naked shoulders. No, he was not alone. He tried to turn his head and look at the mare. That was no good. His head spun and the stars skipped willy-nilly through the heavens. He pulled the Navajo rug close around his shoulders and nestled down amongst the grasses. He shut his eyes and waited in the darkness behind his lids.

When he reopened his eyes, the stars had stopped skipping and were calmly staring back at him. He focused on one star at a time. He was connecting them.

"The little black dots have all gone to white," he said to the dogs and mare. The dogs tilted their heads then resumed cleaning themselves. "It is not as hard as it seems," he continued. "It is not as black with all the stars."

Clem revisited his black fears, the lifelong fears that had encrusted themselves onto him like barnacles to the hull of a ship. He did not have to believe in them. He could scrape them away. He could believe in something else. He might even be able to bend time. The burnt field would not be black forever. It has changed and will continue to change. It will grow green and give birth to forests and feed millions of creatures.

"The dots are lining up pretty damn well," he said aloud. *Change ain't so bad,* he thought. "I'm due for a change," he said. He shivered and managed to make the small familiar lip spitting sound. He could no longer feel his arms or legs.

The dogs had drifted away and were barking alternately in the distance. Clem faded in and out of wakefulness. When he was aware, he would stretch his arm out and touch the tall grass and poke his fingers in the dirt. He would listen to the barks or what sounded like barks. They would fade in and out. He would fade in and out like the breathing of the earth.

"Keep your pants on, I'm coming," he mumbled.

He touched the ground over and over. The field felt good underneath him. He felt that it held him in its arms. It welcomed him.

Clem heard the barks again.

"I know that sound."

*That was it*, he thought, *it's calling me.*

"No one would mind if I stayed here. I know this field."

He thought he felt that crispness in the air that always precedes autumn. Like the brush of air when someone walks by.

But then it was gone.

# About the Author

Peter Edward Burg is a musician and a writer of prose, poetry, songs, and plays. He was raised in Southern California. He is a graduate of University of Colorado at Pueblo and currently resides in Rye, Colorado.

# Middle Creek Publishing Titles

## Fiction

| | |
|---|---|
| Messiah Complex and Other Stories | Michael Olin-Hitt |
| Sphinx | Andrea DeJean |
| The Yellow Field | Peter Edward Burg |

## Poetry

| | |
|---|---|
| Span | David Anthony Martin |
| Deepening the Map | David Anthony Martin |
| Phases | Erika Moss Gordon |
| Cirque & Sky | Kathleen Willard |
| Lessons from Fighting the Black Snake at Standing Rock | Nick Jaina & Leslie Orihel |
| Wild Be | One Leaf |
| Bijoux | David Anthony Martin |
| Sawhorse | Tony Burfield |
| Almost Everything, Almost Nothing | KB Ballentine |
| Kimono Mountain | Mike Parker |
| p a l e o s | Hoag Holmgren |
| I | Bengt O Björklund |
| Across the Light | Bruce Owens |
| Faces of Fishing Creek | Kyle Laws |
| a daughter's aubade | Mara Adamitz Scrupe |
| Secondary Cicatrices | Lynne Goldsmith |
| Unraveling the Endless Sky | Sandra Noel |
| The Ground Nest | David Anthony Martin |
| A Wild Silence | John Noland |
| The Shaman Speaks | Joseph Murphy |
| Erodes on Air | Mark Goodwin |
| Hush | Rosemerry Wahtola Trommer |
| Catchments | E. A. Lechleitner |
| This Incendiary Season | Kathleen Willard |

## Non-Fiction

| | |
|---|---|
| No Better Place: A New Zen Primer | Hoag Holmgren |

# About Middle Creek Publishing

MIDDLE CREEK PUBLISHING believes that responding to the world through art & literature — and sharing that response — is a vital part of being an artist.

MIDDLE CREEK PUBLISHING is a company seeking to make the world a better place through both the means and ends of publishing. We are publishers of quality literature in any genre from authors and artists, both seasoned and as-yet undervalued, with a great interest in works which may be considered to be, illuminate or embody any aspect of contemplative Human Ecology, defined as the relationship between humans and their natural, social, and built environments.

MIDDLE CREEK's particular interest in Human Ecology, is meant to clarify an aspect of the quality in the works we will consider for publication, and is meant as a guide to those considering submitting work to us. Our interest is in publishing works illuminating the Human experience through words, story or other content that connects us to each other, our environment, our history and our potential deeply and more consciously.